Double En

John Leith is an easy-going Edinburgh accountant, a widower with a young son, and a long-standing relationship with an attractive woman which neither wants to turn into marriage.

Suddenly his life is disturbed when he is attacked in his office, his flat searched and vandalized, and his sister's home broken into. John can discern no reason for the incidents, but as the violence against him steps up he begins to feel like a tethered goat and is drawn willy-nilly into the activities of his uncle's detective agency, which seems to offer his best hope of protection, to say nothing of discovering what lies behind these unprovoked attacks.

But when his unknown enemies turn their attention to those who matter most to him, John Leith discovers that he too can use violence when necessary, and Margaret McKinlay's first novel reaches a shattering climax as the identity of the villains and their true motive are finally unmasked.

MARGARET McKINLAY

Double Entry

THE CRIME CLUB
An Imprint of HarperCollins *Publishers*

First published in Great Britain in 1992
by The Crime Club, an imprint of
HarperCollins Publishers, 77–85 Fulham Palace Road,
Hammersmith, London W6 8JB

9 8 7 6 5 4 3 2 1

For my husband Patrick, my children
Frances, Patricia, John, and for James

A catalogue record for this book is
available from the British Library

ISBN 0 00 232381 8

Photoset in Linotron Baskerville by
Rowland Phototypesetting Ltd
Bury St Edmunds, Suffolk
Printed and bound in Great Britain by
HarperCollins Book Manufacturing, Glasgow

PROLOGUE

He was hungry. Hands deep in the pockets of his black bomber jacket, the young man hunched his shoulders against the chill wind and looked around for a café, but it was too early in the morning and nothing was open.

The narrow winding street of the Edinburgh suburb was clogged with slow-moving traffic; he envied the drivers who had spent the night in warm beds, had eaten breakfasts and were now on their way to work. Then he brightened as he saw a familiar face and he darted between cars to cross the street. It was the perfect answer, he wouldn't need to go right across town now. Instead he could head for home, shave and eat, before going to work.

Thirty yards back, a silver BMW had pulled into the kerb and the occupants, hidden from view by smoked glass windows, watched the young man's progress. They noted who he spoke to and then the man in the back seat issued precise orders in a flat tone.

'Pick him up and get the other car to follow that one.'

The young man in the bomber jacket, cheerful now, was not to eat breakfast that day, nor any other day.

CHAPTER 1

Friday began, deceptively, like any other day. John Leith looked from the window of his flat at a grey sky, at litter being blown into shop doorways by a cold November wind, and almost decided not to bother going to work. However, there was young Tracy, already on her way in from Rose-burn, a five-minute bus ride away from his office, so he really had no choice.

He didn't hurry over breakfast—being his own boss, he had no need to reach the office at a certain time. Young Tracy would arrive before him and open the mail, make fresh coffee, and they might discuss her latest boyfriend while she added more gel to support her new spiky hair-do. He'd keep her there for as long as he could, to put off the moment when he had his own day to face, before she collected up any typing he needed done.

Then she went on to her real job in Kramer Property, the office block in the High Street, owned by his uncle, Rees Kramer. It was a convenient arrangement—John didn't have to employ an assistant and Tracy enjoyed her late start to her own day at Kramer's.

She was sixteen, bright and talkative and totally unconcerned by the fact that he was her boss's nephew. Sometimes she made him feel old as she told him about her latest romance while they had coffee. She perched on his desk, swinging her legs, and then with a final smoothing down of her mini-skirt, a manœuvre that gave the morning its sparkle, she would leave around ten—depending on when he got there in the first place.

It was a good way to start any day. It set the tone for the rest of the hours he felt obliged to put in and if he had no appointments he might even drive her to Kramer's and loiter there for an hour or so. But today was to be slightly different because he was to spend the weekend with his sister who looked after his son David. He had a vague plan to leave around lunch-time, arriving at Gwen's home in Biggar in time for afternoon tea.

He switched on the radio in the hope of catching the weather forecast while he gathered up the bits and pieces that he was taking with him, David's birthday present, Gwen's favourite chocolates, his briefcase and suitcase.

'. . . central Scotland down to the Borders may have snow flurries. Drivers are warned to watch out for ice on the the roads . . .' More or less what he'd expected.

Outside it was freezing and he slipped on the icy pavement, scattering his armload of smaller items. As usual, the gritters had not listened to the forecast and the pavements were treacherous.

Everything was slowed down that morning, mainly because he'd caught the worst of the traffic coming in from the Forth Bridge and as always, if the roads to the north were bad, the commuters would be crawling into town. The minutes ticked by as he got stuck in a jam on the steep cobbled street out of Stockbridge, but it didn't bother him because he wasn't on a strict timetable. The car was warming up and he was enjoying a Rush tape—one of Tracy's —and he didn't have a twinge of premonition that anything unusual was about to alter his plans for the day.

He parked in the private space reserved for permit holders outside the elegant Georgian terrace where most of the houses had been converted into offices, then said good morning to the elderly cleaning lady who was polishing the brass plate on the wall of the building. Minutes ticked by as Rachel discussed the weather.

'Too cold for snow, do you think?' she asked, straightening up with one hand supporting her back.

She was long past retiring age but said her little job was all that kept her from stagnating.

'Is it this weekend you visit your boy?'

'Mm. Leaving around lunch-time. It's his birthday tomorrow.'

Rachel had been cleaning the offices for years and she knew the history and habits of every person who worked in the converted Georgian building.

'I've bought him a camera.'

She nodded approvingly. 'Well, you watch yourself, Mr Leith. It's a nasty old road in bad weather.'

And she went back to giving the brass a further polish. There were several names on the plate, including his own which read 'John Leith, accountant', and beside it there was an entry-phone system. He went in through the open glass door, up one flight of carpeted stairs, past two other company offices where people were already at work, then reached his own half-glazed door. He could smell the coffee perking on the small stove in the back room but Tracy was playing one of her favourite heavy metal tapes loudly and she didn't hear him come in, so he stood at his desk and looked through the morning's mail which she had already opened.

He didn't hear the glass door open behind him, nor did he see the intruder who held a short heavy wooden club.

The man didn't hesitate: he brought the weapon down hard on the back of John's head, but some instinct made John move just enough for the blow to be a glancing one. He was still conscious as he fell, long enough to see the frayed ends of jeans and a pair of dirty white trainers and then he sank into a dark painful pit.

His face was deep in carpet pile when he came round and he could smell the stale dustiness of it. There was fluff in his mouth and the taste of the blood that had trickled from the back of his head.

He couldn't understand what had happened and he lay there for some time trying to work it out but in the end he was forced to move because of the acrid smell from the dried-out coffee pot. He lurched towards the small back room that was little more than a cloakroom and bumped against the door frame as his vision blurred. The handle of the pot was hot and he dropped it, but all the liquid had evaporated and the dregs had congealed into a foul mess. Where was Tracy? Close to passing out again, he staggered back into the other room and leaned against his desk, and that was when he saw her lying behind it, sprawled beside his one expensive item of furniture, a soft leather reclining chair.

She was on her back, one arm flung up beside her head, and she was deathly pale.

A red swelling over one eye was pulling her eyebrow upwards and a tiny line of blood had run into her eye socket to create a dark puddle. At first he thought the eye itself was gone and a wave of nausea brought bile into his mouth, but after he'd moved around the desk, leaning on it for support like a drunk, he saw it was not as bad as that. Bad enough, though.

Her mini-skirt had risen up to reveal brief panties under her patterned black tights. Illogically his first instinct was to bend to pull down the skirt, because although the young girl liked to give the impression of being trendy, he knew that she would have been embarrassed by the almost obscene position in which she was lying. But he knew he couldn't possibly bend down without passing out again, so instead he reached for the phone.

The ambulance came almost at the same time as the police and he was again sitting on the floor with his back against the desk when the first uniformed man came through the door.

'Please see to Tracy first. I'm all right,' he said but the words were so carefully pronounced, with lips and tongue like rubber, that now he even sounded like an elegant drunk.

They were very good, both sets of uniforms, and in no time he had given a statement of sorts, had been examined, and was on his way to the Royal Infirmary.

From there someone phoned Rees Kramer, who arrived to find his nephew on a bed in the casualty department, waiting for the results of a head X-ray.

The back of John's neck felt as if it was being pierced by a red-hot shaft of steel but he knew it wouldn't do to let Rees see how badly he felt. Rees wouldn't want to know those details anyway.

'See if you can find out how Tracy is,' he asked his uncle. 'I've asked, but they keep telling me to wait.'

Rees, as usual, looked immaculate in a dark suit and white shirt, regimental tie. His moustache was neatly trimmed and he looked as if he'd just shaved, yet John knew that no real effort was needed to present this image to the world; Rees was just that sort of person.

'I've already asked,' Rees said, lowering himself on to the edge of a moulded plastic chair.

He kept his spine very straight as if to avoid contact with the cheap material. 'They've managed to get hold of her mother, who is on her way here, but a nurse says the girl doesn't appear to be seriously hurt.'

He looked through a gap in the green curtains around the cubicle. 'The doctors are too busy to see anyone, apparently.' Then he turned back to John. 'Did you see the man who hit you?'

The question sounded polite, but it was evident from the sharp expression in his eyes that he was intensely interested.

'I didn't see his face, just his feet,' John murmured as his neck throbbed viciously again. 'I'm not going to stay in here, Rees.'

'You'll do whatever the doctors think best,' his uncle said stiffly and John realized that they were both whispering, as if unseen ears were listening on the other side of the surrounding curtains. Someone was groaning quite close by and hurrying feet in soft-soled shoes squeaked on polished floor tiles; instruments clattered into a steel tray and trolleys swished by, while all around were the soft tones of nurses and doctors in other cubicles and the usual hospital smells.

'I hate bloody hospitals,' John muttered, trying to stop the questions that were zipping through his mind. 'Who hit me and how the hell did he get into the building?' he muttered, trying to lift himself up higher on the pillows. 'And why would anyone want to get into my office?—I don't have anything worth stealing.'

'The police think he slipped in behind you. The cleaning woman was outside apparently and she'd left the doors open. All those offices get visitors and she wasn't to know what he was up to.'

'So much for the security of an entry phone,' John said, resting his head back gingerly on pillows that seemed to be lined with stiff water-proofed material.

'They'll be asking questions and no doubt someone will give a description of him,' Rees said. He shifted on the chair and John realized that his uncle was ill at ease in these surroundings, or perhaps he was just irritated by the need to be there at all. John felt the usual twinge of guilt, that somehow he'd interrupted Rees's plans for the day and that now his uncle was counting the lost minutes. Probably he was entirely wrong, but for as long as he could remember he'd never been able to read his uncle's mind because the man was so private. To make amends, he tried to be constructive.

'Rachel,' he said. 'She must have seen the man.'

Then the curtains were pushed back and a young Chinese lady doctor moved to take his pulse.

'I'm Dr Wu. Your X-ray is all right, no fractures, no need for stitches.' She smiled slightly as if she could hear her own fractured English. 'And you can go as long as you promise to take it easy for a day or two. Head injuries are not to be taken lightly and there is a degree of concussion.'

John assured her that he wouldn't do anything too energetic.

'I'm visiting my sister for a lazy weekend.'

'That would be sensible, but before you leave a policeman wants a word with you.'

And Rees immediately stood up. 'I'll go and see if I can find out anything about Tracy,' he said, and moved smartly through the curtains.

There were two policemen. One looked John over while the other reached into his pocket for a notebook; they both looked as if they did this sort of interview regularly and the questions were perfunctory and a repeat of those John had already answered at his office.

'No, I didn't see the man's face,' he told them. 'And there's nothing worth stealing in my office.'

'Your wallet?' the man asked and John struggled to pat his pockets, then reached in to produce it.

'I don't think there's anything missing,' he said, flicking through the compartments. 'That's strange, surely?'

But the policeman with the notebook snapped it shut and tucked it back into his pocket.

'He was disturbed by your young lady and both she and the cleaning woman got a good look at him.'

Relief flooded through John. 'Tracy's all right, then?'

The man nodded. 'A bump on the head. She'll be fine. She says he was bent over you when she came from the back room and he lashed out at her. She probably scared the shit out of him and he acted without thinking, but she was very lucky to get off so lightly. Even so, they're keeping her in overnight. We got the best description from the old girl, the cleaner.' And now the policemen exchanged amused glances. 'She said he had a big bum, that it "caught your eye because the rest of him wasn't fat". Actually, that's the sort of detail that is really helpful . . . now we just have to find a five-foot-ten villain with a big bum.' And they left with a promise to let him know what developed, but John thought they didn't sound too hopeful.

Rees came back after the constables had left. 'The girl's going to be all right. Look, why go to Gwen's? Come to Elmwood for the weekend.'

'Because I promised David I'd be there for his birthday,' John said. 'Let's get out of here.' His legs felt shaky as he went with Rees to the car, and his head felt as if it would be easily disconnected from his neck, so he didn't argue when Rees drove to the High Street, to the rear of the Kramer building where there was private parking for the staff. They took the lift to the small flat that Rees had on the top floor which they both used quite often. There was only a large bedroom with a double bed, a small sitting-room, a kitchen and a bathroom, but Rees had furnished it with nice pieces and the décor was discreet, in Rees's style. The carpets were thick and the flat was so high above the street that the traffic sounds were hardly noticeable. It was a haven that Rees often used when he decided not to go home to Elmwood, his country house, and John kept spare clothes there so that he could change if he was going out for the evening and didn't want to rush home.

'I'll make some coffee,' Rees said.

'And I'll get changed—the blood has dried on the back of this shirt and it's rubbing my neck.'

'Do you always dress like that for work?' Rees wore a

slight frown which was a distinct mark of disapproval, and John shrugged and looked down at his jeans.

'It's comfortable and makes the clients feel comfortable.' Rees sniffed.

John took the time to shower too, and as he dried himself he noticed how gloomy the room was. He walked to the window that was several floors above the busy street below, looked at the sky and wondered if David would be disappointed if he couldn't get out with his birthday camera.

'Coffee's ready,' Rees said from the doorway. 'How's your head?'

He was a tall man with an erect carriage, in his early sixties, and had the pink complexion that went well with his short silver hair. He had an air of success about him, but the expensive suits that sat well on his shoulders had nothing to do with the aura that Rees had. It was something that oozed out of the man, an elusive trait of character that spelled confidence in himself and inspired it in others. He wore his wealth like an overcoat but never made a show of it. He had great charm with clients but also had a rigid reserve that masked the inner core of the man.

John respected him as the man who had not shirked his duty when John's parents disappeared on a sailing holiday. There was never any question that Rees should be given due respect, but love was a different matter. It had not been easy for a ten-year-old boy because Rees had never pretended to be fatherly, had never attempted to be any more than a caring guardian. There had always been an unspoken agreement that Rees had his own life, valued his privacy, but would provide material comforts, and that he'd done generously. There had never been any great feeling of closeness between them although they'd shared the same house for ten years.

'My neck's stiff, that's all,' John assured him as he reached for the strong black coffee. 'It'll be a bit uncomfortable driving but it's not bad enough to cancel my weekend.'

Rees nodded. 'Then you'd better get something to eat—we've missed our lunch. Tollis and I were going to meet for a pub lunch and they'll still be serving—I'll phone and see if he's in his office.'

The Sentinel Agency was the other half of Rees's business, situated in the same building, although clients used a separate door leading in from the High Street. Tollis managed it now that Rees was cutting back on work, 'semiretired' he said, although he seemed as busy as ever.

'He says he's busy but he'll come,' Rees grunted. 'You can tell him exactly what happened.'

Tollis ran his side of the business with only a little interference from Rees and the three of them discussed the intruder at John's office as they ate.

Tollis, taciturn as usual, said, 'These opportunist crimes are on the increase in the city. Drugs. Addicts take chances out of desperation, when other criminals wouldn't risk it. Your man chanced his luck, John—he wanted anything of value that he could carry easily and he would hit anyone in his way. And they don't bother to wait for darkness any more. You were in the wrong place at the wrong time. Put it out of your mind.'

He spoke as if he knew what he was talking about, but John, who had grown up knowing that Rees owned Sentinel, had never been interested enough to ask what Sentinel did.

Tollis was a man of the same height as Rees but was much heavier, dark in colouring and entirely different in nature.

He was a man of few words who had none of Rees's charm; a loner who seemed to shun close friendships, and although it had registered, John hadn't given much thought to why he'd never heard the man's first name, not even from Rees. It was always just Tollis.

And as if to prove that he couldn't waste time on something that only the police could solve, Tollis was impatient to get back to work.

'We've got a bit of an emergency on and I must be there when the men come in.'

Rees's head jerked up at that, but Tollis laid a restraining hand on his partner's shoulder.

'Nothing for you to bother about, Rees,' he said bluntly.

'And I think I should get on the road,' John said. 'The food has helped shift the headache and I don't want to get caught up in rush-hour traffic.'

'That reminds me,' Rees said, reaching down to pick up his briefcase. 'I want you to take a look at some clients' files—you could entertain them over the next few weeks, perhaps. If you've time over the weekend . . . ?'

He opened the case and handed John some slim folders as they left the pub. The one on top said Mr H. Carrick.

'Carrick?' John had heard Rees mention the name but he couldn't connect it with any land deal.

Rees looked annoyed for a moment. 'I told the girl to take that one out . . . there's some sort of hold-up and it's not likely to go ahead.'

John had never seen Rees so uncomfortable, so he flipped through the other files, recognizing some of the names. It was one of the perks of having a wealthy uncle that sometimes he got to entertain the clients because Rees hated one-to-one contact over a dinner table—another of his foibles.

They were walking three abreast along the pavement when Trollis paused, his brow puckered with a frown.

'Carrick . . . didn't he get the Sinclair estate by marrying the widow?'

'That's him,' Rees agreed dourly. 'John won't remember the weekends I used to spend there when Graham Sinclair was alive . . .'

Tollis interrupted again as he remembered something. 'I got one of the men to collect your car, by the way, John. It's round the back.'

It wasn't really John's car because he didn't own one, but simply used any of the Kramer cars that was free. He made his way around the rear of the building to collect it and he didn't notice the two men in the car parked across the street who had been watching and were now ready to follow him when he left.

CHAPTER 2

Rees walked to the Sentinel office with Tollis. 'John seems to have taken all that very well,' he murmured with a slight frown. 'Surprising, really.'

Tollis shrugged, his mind already on other things.

'What's the emergency?' Rees went on, and Tollis turned and shook his head.

'You can't keep away, can you, Rees? Retired my foot!' He hesitated and then jerked his head. 'Well, maybe you should hear what I have to say at that. Some of the men will be in by now.'

It was not Tollis's office that they entered, but the long narrow room where the men were assigned their work each day. The room wasn't large, and was crowded now with eight men sitting in any available seat and others perched on desks or leaning against the walls. A couple wore the blue uniform with the Sentinel flash over the breast pocket, others were in dark suits.

Most of them had come from the police force or the services and the discipline was still stamped on them, like an invisible uniform of a different kind.

The majority were young and fit, with the short haircuts that they had grown used to and were encouraged to keep. They followed Tollis with their eyes as he made his way through them to the desk at the top, their expressions alert. It was obvious from the smokey atmosphere that they had been waiting for some time, fidgeting with impatience. Rees joined Tollis but stayed behind him, and he noticed that one of the older men, Mike Cairns, was in the front row. Mike was an old hand and a personal friend but now he seemed unaware of Rees and kept his eyes fixed on Tollis.

He was bent forward, resting his elbows on his thighs and his large hands were clasped so tightly that the flesh of his fingers was white. Rees looked uneasy. He recognized the signs of anxiety and turned to watch as Tollis leaned across the desk and murmured softly to Mike, who seemed to be insisting that he intended to stay. Tollis shrugged and glanced through the papers on his desk before starting to speak.

'As you've probably heard, we have lost touch with Mike's young son, Toby,' he said slowly. Tollis never revealed any emotion and his tone was flat. Rees glanced at Mike Cairns with alarm as Tollis went on.

'Toby is a new employee, a bit uncertain of the need to keep in touch, perhaps, but Mike is concerned so I want everyone to ask around. Use any contacts you have and let us know if you hear anything.' There was no mistaking that he meant exactly what he said and all those listening knew that Tollis was understating his anxiety.

For a few moments no one moved and then they slowly began to file out, but Mike remained and he looked angry.

'Is that it? That's all you've got to say to them?' He turned and appealed to Rees, but Rees said nothing.

Tollis sighed. 'Go home, Mike—Toby may phone you.'

'If he does it'll be here. He knows I'll be at work.'

'OK. You can co-ordinate any information that comes in but let's not start imagining things yet.'

Mike jumped to his feet and his face was red with anger. 'I didn't imagine his phone call. I said I'd keep quiet about the job he was on, but surely the men should have been told what he was doing?'

Tollis looked startled and puzzled. 'But he wasn't, Mike. I would never send someone as raw as Toby out on his own.'

Mike pointed an accusing finger at Rees. 'Well, *he* did. He sent Toby to Gumley's house.'

'What?' The word was an angry hiss, and Tollis too turned to stare at Rees. 'Is that true?'

Rees's face was set but he nodded.

'There was no danger. I simply wanted to keep an eye on the place and report any comings and goings.'

Mike was looking from one to the other. 'You did this off your own bat, Rees? What the hell's going on here?'

Tollis sensed that Mike was about to explode and he tried to calm the situation. He laid a hand on Mike's arm and spoke quietly to him.

'I'll talk to Rees and get the full story—there's just been a cock-up in orders. I'll get back to you when Rees and I have sorted it all out—you take incoming calls in the meantime.' He was edging Mike towards the door as he spoke and the discipline that was part of the man took over and he did as Tollis asked, but before he went out he shot a glance in Rees's direction that was both angry and disgusted.

Tollis marched past Rees into his own office and once Rees was inside he slammed the door. 'Now perhaps you'll tell me what the hell is going on.'

It was a large room, quite like Rees's own but here there was evidence of the amount of work that the agency had to handle. Files were piled high on the desk and the walls were lined with cabinets, some with drawers open on crammed-in files. Dirty coffee cups and full ashtrays littered a small table and the air was stale. Tollis threw open a window and a freezing draught sent papers fluttering to the floor.

'Well?' Tollis snapped as he scooped the papers up and slammed them on the desk.

Rees was pale and his eyes seemed to have sunk into shadowy sockets but he still protested that Toby couldn't have come to any harm at Albert Gumley's home. 'He was just to watch and report back,' he said.

Tollis couldn't keep still. He paced as Rees spoke and

then turned on his partner. 'Report *what*, for God's sake? Are we still in the service, Rees, still playing little secret games?'

Rees hesitated. 'I know we agreed not to do any more jobs for Special Branch but this seemed like a couple-of-days affair—there was a rumour that Gumley was back in action and there's been a flood of heroin in circulation.' He seemed to lose confidence in what he was saying as he went along, as if Tollis's anger had shocked him.

Tollis stooped and leaned on his desk, taking all his weight on his spread hands. 'Tell me again what Special Branch wanted, Rees,' he said coldly.

Rees lowered himself into a soft leather chair and he seemed to shrink at the same time. His shoulders became rounded and his hands shook slightly. Tollis had never seen Rees like this before and that made him all the more concerned.

'It was all very vague,' he said.

Tollis snorted. 'Gumley was never involved in drugs and he's been confined to that house of his for years. John told me that he was slowly dying—why the hell would that man suddenly risk everything he's stacked away?'

Rees's head came up at the mention of John's name and a gleam of hope crept into his eyes. 'John could go to Gumley and find out about Toby,' he said, but Tollis dismissed the suggestion with a wave of his hand.

'And what would he say—"please could you tell Rees what has happened to the man he sent to spy on you"? Besides, Gumley may be John's father-in-law but John can't stand the man. We all know that he never goes near him willingly, except to comply with that custody agreement he made regarding young David. Gumley would smell a rat and right now I don't want him knowing that Toby works for me.' Tollis emphasized every word with a stabbing finger.

'He'll be all right. He's young and inexperienced,' Rees said. 'He was desperately keen to work here like his father . . . maybe Toby doesn't realize how important it is to keep to schedules. He could have a girl, could have gone off somewhere . . .' But Rees knew he was clutching at any hope and Tollis didn't even answer.

Tollis suddenly leaned forward and stared directly at Rees. 'Something stinks. I have a gut feeling about this . . . that young Toby is in trouble. It was drummed into him how important it was to phone in if he couldn't get to work and last night he called his father and said he was on his way home. Mike says he sounded agitated but he didn't think anything of it until he failed to turn up.' Tollis suddenly thumped his desk with his fist and more papers spilled on to the floor but he ignored them and turned his back on Rees.

'He's only twenty-two,' he said softly. 'And my guts tell me he's in real trouble. Your fault. He should never have been sent there and if anything's happened to that young man I hope you live with it for the rest of your life.'

CHAPTER 3

For John, who knew nothing of the drama at Sentinel, the weekend passed quickly, but apart from the underlying uneasiness about the incident in his office, he now had a new problem to face and he needed space to think. So on that Monday morning he slipped out early while it was still dark, dressed in an old jogging suit that he kept at Gwen's. He had long ago discovered that once his feet found a rhythm he could shut everything out except the thing he wanted to concentrate on.

It was too dark to take to the open country so he ran in the streets, on pavements that were gritted against the ice and at first he found it hard going. He was out of condition and the cold air nipped at his face and ears but as his body warmed, the stiffness eased and he began to relish the sheer exhilaration of running again.

He let the rhythm take over and turned his thoughts to the conversation he'd had the previous evening with his sister.

After David was in bed, Gwen had dropped her bombshell.

'We need to talk,' she said. And John thought that she was going to raise the old theme of 'after seven years, wasn't it time he thought of re-marrying?'

She was seventeen when their parents disappeared on a sailing holiday, seven years older than he was, and she'd assumed the rôle of mother figure. John suspected that she resented Rees taking that authority away from her at the time but there was nothing she could have done about it. So now at thirty-nine, she still sometimes tried to set his life to rights. They'd been over the question of marriage several times although she'd never gone as far as asking if he was celibate. Maybe that was on the agenda this time? But he was wrong.

'It's about David,' she said, and immediately John felt a familiar twinge of guilt. Gwen had taken David into her home when he was a baby of four weeks old and at that time John had felt nothing more than relief. For the first years he'd been content to be a visiting father, but gradually guilt had replaced the relief and as if she could read his thoughts, Gwen spoke gently.

'My own three are settled in boarding-school and Greg wants me to sell up here and join him in Aberdeen. He's tired of us being separated for weeks on end and the move wouldn't make any difference to our boys. They'd come to us in the holidays as usual, but David's a different matter. We feel . . .' she hesitated. 'Greg says I should ask you if you want to make a home for David.'

'Mm.' John let his breath out in a long sigh and Gwen quickly went on.

'He could always board like my three, or be a day boy. There's no rush to decide,' she said anxiously. 'And to be honest I'll weep buckets because he's like my own son. Greg is right, though—it has to be your decision.'

He hadn't expected this. Somehow the future had stretched ahead much the same as it was now, with David growing up happily with Gwen.

'I don't know anything about being a father,' he said, which was very true. 'And David is always so polite that I feel more like his uncle—you must have noticed how he is with me. Wouldn't it turn his life upside down to move him now?'

'The only alternative is to take him to Aberdeen,' she reminded him, and John knew he didn't want that. It wasn't fair on Gwen for a start, but he realized that he didn't like the idea of not seeing his son regularly either.

'Maybe you should ask him,' Gwen said. 'I know he's only seven but he may know exactly what he wants.'

John had looked around the comfortable room which was almost shabby in its comfort. Gwen had never been interested in smart décor and the furniture showed the knocks of rough handling by four growing boys. The bungalow had an acre of garden that was trampled by football and rugby, and Gwen herself had the comfortable roundness that came from a contented life, while he had a small flat and no idea of how to be a father to a seven-year-old boy.

'Just think about it,' his sister urged. She didn't nag, although in the past she had made it plain that she despaired of the way he'd lost all impetus in life after his wife was killed. It had been very easy for him to take each day as it came, letting others make the decisions.

Lights were coming on in the houses of the little market town. A milk-float hummed by and some early commuters quietly left their homes, closing doors on families still asleep. The world was waking up as he headed back to breakfast, his breath streaming out in a condensed cloud while sweat trickled down inside his tracksuit.

He would have to look for a house, he'd decided, and home help. He couldn't provide all that Gwen hoped for— certainly not a mother-figure, and that was the one aspect that she hadn't mentioned. Maybe she knew of the existence of Clare Aitken and the unconventional affair that had lasted for three years, and guessed that in that respect he had a different problem.

How would Clare react to having a young child thrust into their lives? What difference was it going to make? He had no idea. And how did you ask your son if he'd like to live with you when you'd never been able to reach out to hug him? There were no rough and tumble games, no physi-

cal contact at all—David never even reached for his hand
when they were out together. The years of partial separ-
ation had put a barrier between them and he didn't know
how to cross it. In the last few years, when fatherly feelings
had finally come to the surface, he admitted to himself that
he'd been afraid that his child would flinch away from
him and had even felt jealous when he saw how easy the
relationship was between David and Greg. Greg had been
the natural father-figure and perhaps David had become
confused by the two male adults in his life. Who could
blame him?

Gwen was grilling bacon. He could smell it as he went
up the path of the house and the juices ran in his mouth.

'I'll have a quick shower,' he said, popping his head
around the kitchen door and she nodded. She knew where
he'd been, and why.

'You know, David has been asking questions lately,' she
said as they ate. 'We've never made a secret of why he lives
with us but he's obviously been thinking about it. And little
boys don't miss much.'

'Does he talk about Trish as well?'

'Of course. He has photographs of her and I know he
talks to his grandfather about her.'

'Gumley won't be able to tell him much,' John said
angrily. 'He hardly saw anything of Trish after his wife
walked out on him.'

'Maybe the old man has forgotten those days. You only
remember the bits you want to remember.'

John pushed away his plate. Gwen didn't know all of
Albert Gumley's background and she tended to see good in
everyone. He changed the subject.

'I'll have a talk with David before I go—I had intended
leaving right after lunch but we'll see how it goes.'

'I heard the forecast and it isn't good. There's snow
sweeping down from the north,' she said as she got up to

clear the table and John went to look at the heavy sky.

'How much film have you got left?' he asked David later. It turned out that most of the spare spools that he'd bought to go with the camera had been used up, so they walked to the shops to buy more and to put the others in to be developed. And as they walked, David skipped ahead with the camera hanging from a strap around his wrist. His legs were long and out of proportion to the rest of his body, showing that he might one day match his father's height, and he had John's dark colouring.

There was hardly any physical resemblance to his mother, but he had a lot of her mannerisms: her easy laughter, a way of tilting his head when he was thinking, and sudden spells of quietness when nothing could distract him from what he was doing. And he had Trish's eye for detail and colour; John realized that it was only lately that he'd even noticed that his wife lived on in their son. And he'd felt cheated. They could have had a proper family life if a drunk hadn't driven up on to the pavement . . .

'David, Aunty Gwen and I were wondering if you'd like to go to school with your cousins,' he said as they walked back to the house. David didn't seem surprised by the question and he even paused to zip up his camera bag carefully.

'Joseph asked me that in the summer holidays but I didn't know if you'd let me,' he said with a shrug.

'What made you think that?'

David looked up at him thoughtfully. 'Because then you'd have no one to visit except Uncle Rees.' He chewed the inside of his cheek before going on and his expression was quite serious. 'But Joe thought you probably had lots of friends in Edinburgh.'

The fact that his son had discussed it all with his cousin and considered he might be lonely made John feel guiltier than ever. He didn't know his son at all.

'I do have friends but I'd like to know how you feel about

the school—whether you'd like to live in a house with me, or board with the boys.'

'Would your house have a garden? Grandfather promised to buy me a puppy for Christmas.'

Again Albert Gumley intruded on a conversation and John cursed the man. 'Does he still phone you regularly?' he asked and David nodded.

'But he sounds awful sick. Will we be going to see him at Christmas?'

'I expect so.' The visiting days had been stipulated and agreed to when Gumley gave up his fight for custody of his grandson. Not that he'd had a chance in hell of winning, but the old man liked to make trouble and in the end John had agreed to take David on regular visits to keep the peace. Anyway, David seemed to like the old man. And in the future there would be the problem of David inheriting the old man's wealth; when the time came it would be up to John to explain where Gumley's money had come from.

'Let's go to the garage to look at some cars,' David said suddenly. He'd never thought much of the ones from Kramer's that John drove. And for the next half-hour they admired the selection that filled the large window space, with prices that would buy a small family home. David pressed his nose against the glass and pointed out details that showed he knew the various makes.

For a while John forgot the problems of the future, of telling Clare that he was about to be a real father. In rare companionship he and David discussed the merits of each model until it came home to him that other fathers had moments like this every day. But they hadn't abandoned their sons when they were only weeks old . . .

A few snowflakes drifted down as they walked back towards the bungalow, with the matter of boarding-school apparently settled. And suddenly David pointed. 'Those men are breaking into your car,' he said, running ahead of John with his arms pumping like mad.

'Wait, David!' John shouted, but his son didn't pause. He reached the men seconds before John and was brushed roughly aside by a man standing beside the open boot. The other man was looking back at John and at the same time edging towards another car parked in front of his own. John ignored both of them and reached instead for David who had fallen heavily to the pavement. He heard the sound of their running feet and the engine of their car start up, but was more concerned about the trickle of blood on David's forehead. Only later did it occur to him that they were hardly the types to own a BMW.

'They're getting away,' David said, his body stiff with the desire to get free to chase them again, but John held him tightly against his chest.

'There's nothing worth stealing, son,' he said. His heart was thudding with the shock of how quickly it had all happened and the fact that David could have been seriously hurt instead of suffering only a graze.

Gwen was equally shocked that it could happen in their quiet street and John knew what she meant. A strange car would stand out and the street was a dead end with only a row of bungalows on the edge of the village. There was no passing traffic, no temptation to attract car thieves. She reached up to inspect David'd injury but he drew back and put his free arm around his father's neck.

'We could have chased them in your car,' he murmured, then he leaned back and grinned. 'But I don't suppose we'd have caught them.'

'Neither do I,' John agreed. 'Let's forget it. Kramer's can afford a new lock for the boot.' They went in to eat lunch with David still clasping John's neck tightly, a new experience that John felt might be the turning-point for him and David, but Gwen was keen to phone the police.

'These things happen,' John told her. 'I didn't get a good look at them or think to note the number of their car.' That was true, but not the real reason why he was not keen on calling the police.

He was vaguely uneasy that this incident should come so soon after an intruder had entered his office and he wanted to discuss it all with Tollis.

Flurries of snow continued on and off during the afternoon but by four it was getting very dark and John decided it would be wise to leave before the weather got any worse. Gwen was satisfied that the question of David's future was settled and John could see that already her thoughts were busy with the move to join Greg in Aberdeen.

She and David stood in the doorway to see him off and he lifted a hand in farewell as the snow fell like a curtain between them. It also hid the car that slipped out of a side road to fall in behind him as he left Biggar, driving with a treacherous inch of snow on top of ice under his wheels.

On the radio he got boys with falsetto voices singing carols, but no weather report, so he switched it off and noted the flash of the headlights of a car behind him. It disappeared now and then as the road twisted around the bends but it appeared to be keeping at a safe distance. John let his thoughts drift to Clare Aitken. He should have phoned her over the weekend but what he had to discuss would need to be face to face.

He wondered what Tollis would have to say about the men forcing the boot of his car—in the wrong place at the wrong time? Surely it was too much of a coincidence that he should twice be the victim of small-time crooks in a short space of time? Yet logic told him that it was probably the case.

There was very little traffic on the road and he was making good time despite the appalling conditions. The snow was a blizzard now, driving at his windscreen like a swarm of angry bees, but he should make Edinburgh with plenty of time to bathe and change before nipping up to Clare's flat.

He was blinded suddenly by the flash of full headlights in his mirror and he inched over to let the driver pass him. Idiot, trying to speed in this weather, but the other car didn't pass. Instead it sat on his tail for a mile and then again indicated that it was overtaking by drawing along-side. John slowed, glancing angrily across at the other vehicle, but to his surprise the passenger seemed to be making motions that he should pull over. It was difficult to be sure because the car's side window was caked with snow, so he slowed further. The other car matched the manœuvre and edged closer still, almost forcing John on to the verge.

'What the hell does he think he's doing?' John accelerated and got his nose in front. 'And I'm staying here, mate,' he muttered. If the other madman fancied meeting a car coming the other way that was his lookout.

The other car fell back but not far and soon John could see it edging up on him again. The passenger was making urgent signals that he should pull over, pointing at the verge and mouthing words that could not be heard. And suddenly John recognized the anger in the expression, which was the same as on the face of the man who had pushed David out of his way earlier that day.

'Christ,' he said. Then he was at a side road, almost went past it, but managed to spin the wheel at the last moment. The car lunged from side to side until he got it back under control and then he was heading down a narrow road to God knows where, but the other car was still on the main road and for the moment he had got away from it. Relief was short-lived as he wondered if it would double back and come after him. What the hell had they wanted from him?

He tried to get his breathing under control while keeping an eye on his mirror at the same time. The verges rose steeply on each side of the road and long spikes of vegetation poked through the snow covering. The fence posts that ran along the top had little caps of snow. The roads's lower level meant it was more sheltered and the blizzard had eased somewhat but even so it was difficult to see where he was heading.

Still no sign of following headlights and he began to think he'd got away from them. He looked for lights or other signs of habitation, but then the road began to bend to the right and the verge on his left gave way to trees with a dark area below them that the snow had not managed to penetrate.

'It's got to go somewhere,' he muttered, looking for a clutch of cottages or a farm. What he really hoped for was a hamlet with a pub, a glass of Scotch and a warm fire, a haven in fact. He admitted to being scared and out of his depth in something that he didn't understand.

The road was still going around a long bend and his neck felt stiff with the tension of peering forward. Still trees on his left and the high bank on his right, with no sign of life anywhere. He glanced in his mirror and with a lurch of his heartbeat he saw the other car coming up fast without lights. It didn't slow at all and suddenly he was thrown forward against his seat-belt as it rammed him. His car went into a skid that he managed to control but then the other car was coming again. This time he was tense with the expectation of it and the shock of the collision jolted his neck.

They were no longer asking him to pull over, they were ordering him to stop or else, but the choice was no longer his to make.

The last collision had caught the rear of his car at an angle and it was now swinging slowly out of control towards the dark area under the trees. He hit a tree which stopped the skid with a sickening jolt, but now he was going over a drop backwards and it was like being swallowed as the bonnet came up and the back end fell into space. The sound of crumbling metal was still in his ears when he bounced off another tree and he flung his arms up around his head.

They couldn't have meant this to happen, John was thinking illogically. They had wanted his wallet, not his death; more muscle than brain, damn them whoever they were. His body was jerked savagely as he bounced off trees and he felt his teeth bite into his lip and tasted blood. The noise was of screeching metal, branches being torn from trees, and the thud of his heartbeat was in his throat and threatening to choke him. Something came loose in the car and struck him on the forehead but he felt no pain. His main concern was how far would he fall? Would he survive?

He lost all sense of direction as the car was buffeted from one direction to another at the whim of the trees in its path. His jaw was clenched tight as were his eyes, and his face ached with the grimace of terror.

There was a pause and the car began to move forward now, angled steeply downwards, and he knew he had to see what lay ahead. He looked through his arms and saw that, incredibly, his headlights were still working. Then he wished he hadn't looked, because dead ahead was the branch of a tree, coming at the windscreen like a spear.

'Oh, fuck . . .'

CHAPTER 4

He was only half conscious when strong arms lifted him into a vehicle up on the road.

'Watch it, Tim, we don't know if he's broken anything.'

'Can't help that. He'll die of cold if we don't get him back to the pub soon.'

The next John knew, he was lying on a hard sofa that smelled of wet dogs and stale beer and a fat lady was wrapping him in blankets. He was aware of other people in the background and the heat coming from a fire but most of all he was glad he was still alive.

'Thank you,' he said and then a tall man in a tweed jacket bent over him, smelling of whisky and tobacco.

'I'm Patrick Robertson. I'm a vet but I could do some stitches in that cut if you like . . . stitching's the same for man or beast. Can you move all your bits?'

John flexed his arms and legs and although he ached as if he'd been badly beaten, nothing seemed to be broken.

'I think my bits are all right,' he said. There was a general sigh of relief from the spectators standing in the doorway with pints of their hands and they stayed on to watch the surgery.

'You won't need a local—you're still in shock, shouldn't feel a thing.'

But he did. Not only did he feel every stab of the curved needle but also the skin of his forehead being pulled together as the knots were tied, and all the time the vet gave a commentary about how lucky he'd been.

'If that tree hadn't hooked your car as neatly as a salmon on a gaff you'd have gone fifty feet over the drop right into the river. Fellow did that last year. It didn't kill him outright, but he drowned—isn't that right, Betty?' The fat lady made a face behind the vet's back as he cleaned away dried blood with a swab and then pressed on a dressing. 'Now then,' the man went on. 'How many fingers do you see?' And he held up two in a rude gesture. John grinned and told him exactly what he saw. 'And do you know who you are?'

'John Leith.'

'He'll do. You can bring him a Scotch and top up my glass as well.'

The fat lady pushed him aside. 'I'll do no such thing. He'll have soup.'

And she sat down on the edge of the sofa and reached to help him sit up in stages, so that he found his head resting on her bosom which was as soft as a cushion and that allowed him to swing his legs to the floor. He pushed aside the blankets because the fire was sending out a fierce heat and saw that he'd lost his shoes and his jeans and sweater were torn and bloodstained. The crowd in the doorway drifted off now that the interesting business of stitching was over and soon he heard the thud of darts hitting a dart board.

The vet had moved to stand with his back to the fire, with one hand holding a glass of Scotch and the other spread behind him to catch the heat of the fire. He had sandy hair that was receding, a ruddy complexion, and the bluest eyes that John had ever seen.

'No point in calling out a doctor tonight but you should have a proper check done tomorrow. No double vision, I suppose.'

John shook his head and that was a mistake. A wave of pain gripped his head in a vice and he shut his eyes until it eased. When he opened them the vet was wincing in sympathy.

'I'll leave you a couple of painkillers. Betty will give you a bed for the night.'

'Where am I—I don't know this area, and what time is it?' John asked.

'Altford and it's just after ten.'

Rees would be worried . . . and he'd promised to phone Gwen.

'Can I use the phone?'

'Soup first,' Betty said at his elbow.

He didn't argue. And it was wonderfully hot and full of vegetables, the best he'd ever tasted although it stung his swollen lip. 'How did anyone know I was down there?' he asked when she took the bowl away.

'Ian from the farm was across the river. He saw the headlights as your car went over but it took him some time to get back here to raise the alarm. Luckily our Tim is daft on climbing so he has the ropes and things.'

So he'd been lucky not to have been trapped in the car all night.

'I'm very grateful to them,' he said quietly. Words weren't really enough.

'Now you can phone your friends,' Betty said with a smile. She wanted to take his arm as they walked to the private rooms down the hall and he was surprised at how shaky he felt. Then he remembered promising the Chinese doctor that he'd have a quiet weekend and he felt a smile stretch his cut lip. Betty left him alone as he dialled Rees's number.

'I slid off the road, Rees,' he said. 'Don't worry, I'm all right, just bruised.'

'We guessed that something had happened,' his uncle said. His voice boomed down the phone. 'Gwen phoned but I'll call her back. Ice, was it?'

John hesitated. He didn't want to go into detail on the phone about the other car, but Rees had to know some time. 'Not exactly. There was another car involved and I ended up going off the road—it wasn't . . . Look, let's leave the explanations until I see you.'

Rees hadn't interrupted and when John finished speaking there was silence for a long moment. And when Rees did speak it was with deliberation. 'Are you saying it wasn't an accident? A skid?'

John sighed. 'To be honest, I'm not sure what it was. The driver of the other car rammed me when I wouldn't pull over. I don't think he meant it to develop the way it did, but on the other hand he doesn't seem to have stopped to report what happened.'

'Were there any witnesses?'

'I don't think so. No one here has mentioned seeing the other car.'

'Good. I'll send someone to fetch you and I'd rather you didn't mention the other car if anyone should ask.'

John wanted to ask Rees why the secrecy, but he was not inclined to argue. He would report it when he got to Edinburgh, but he certainly didn't want to face making statements tonight. 'OK, but don't send a car tonight. I'm in a pub in Altford and the landlady has got a bed for me. To be honest, I'd like to fall into it very soon.'

'You sure you're all right?' Rees asked sharply.

'I'm sure. Send a car in the morning.' John put the phone down and sat in the quiet room for a few more moments, thinking about the intruder in his office and now the events of this day. What on earth was going on?

Betty was back, her round face beaming. She looked the type to make an excellent landlady. 'Finished?' She came right in then and looked apologetic. 'There's a policeman would like a word . . . he's not official, he just lives here, but he says that it will save you giving a statement in the morning if he has a chat with you now.'

John thought about the waiting bed and then got up stiffly.

'OK.'

He followed her back to the lounge where a man in his late forties was sitting in one of the comfortable armchairs beside the fire. He had neatly cut dark hair, heavy dark eyebrows and was wearing a cream roll-necked sweater over brown cords. A black Labrador sat beside his chair and he was fondling its ears.

'Mr Leith? . . . Robert Jamieson,' he said, holding out his hand.

John sat opposite him and asked Betty if he could have a small Scotch. And while she was fetching it, the two men studied each other. Jamieson didn't look like a village bobby, and remembering what Rees had said, John wondered how he could answer this man's questions without mentioning the other car. Couldn't policemen tell when two cars collided from the marks left on the road? He decided he was too tired to care.

'I expect you feel like a soak in the tub to ease your aches, so I won't keep you long. I was once in a minor accident myself so I can guess how you're feeling.' He was brisk and friendly but his eyes had an intelligent gleam that warned John to be careful about what he said, although he wasn't sure why he was supposed to withhold part of his story. No doubt Rees had his reasons.

'I came along that way tonight,' the policeman said. 'The trees give the road quite a bit of shelter but the blizzard was bad around the time you went over the edge—you hadn't been drinking, Mr Leith?'

John hadn't been expecting that. 'No,' he said vehemently.

The policeman smiled. 'I'm not on duty and I'll take your word. But I'm puzzled and I'll admit it. This road is hardly well used unless by the local residents—so where were you going?'

'I know the main road well because I visit my sister regularly—in Biggar.' He'd fallen into a trap and now he had to explain why he left the main road. 'I didn't feel too good so I came off the road for a break. I hurt my head the other day and I must still be suffering from the after-effects.' He was getting in deeper.

'Another accident?' Jamieson said with a hint of amusement.

'A bump on the head, nothing serious,' John said shortly. Now he knew how the police got their information out of people; they just sat back and let fools babble on.

Jamieson let it rest. 'So you were visiting your sister. Then heading for Edinburgh, I presume?'

'That's right.'

The dog lifted its head and stared up at his master every time he spoke and the policeman was still stroking its head. It was a beautiful dog, with a well-groomed coat that gleamed.

John took a sip of whisky and rolled it around his tongue before swallowing it and then he felt the heat of it spread through his body. He sipped again. Jamieson seemed to relax, took out a pipe and lit it and then sank back deeper into his chair.

'I like Edinburgh but I prefer to live here. Do you live in the city, Mr Leith?'

'I've a flat in Stockbridge.' Now the man would ask if he was married, but instead the policeman shifted direction and asked where John worked. 'I'm an accountant.' That was safe enough. 'I have an office in the West End.' He was getting tired of the probing questions, for he was aware that was what Jamieson was doing. Did he already suspect that John was holding something back?

'I think I'd like to get to bed now,' he said, starting to rise.

'Of course. Is there anyone I can contact for you?'

'No, I've already phoned my uncle,' John said. 'Rees Kramer. He's got a business in the High Street.'

John didn't know why he added that last piece of information, except that usually it forestalled having to explain that yes, it was *the* Rees Kramer of Kramer Property, but it certainly had an effect on the policeman who was now standing. He was several inches short of John's six feet two but the man had a presence that made him seem equal in height.

'I know Mr Kramer,' he said, his eyes alert now, and there was something else that looked like suspicion. 'It changes things a bit, doesn't it? The people who work for your uncle seem to be prone to accidents,' and he emphasized the last word.

'Perhaps you'll tell him that we met,' he went on abruptly. 'Tell him Chief Inspector Robert Jamieson sends his regards—I think he'll be interested.'

And with a snap of his fingers to the dog the policeman left the room.

'Now what the hell was that about?' John muttered. It was as if the man automatically disbelieved his story—only when he mentioned the name of Kramer.

CHAPTER 5

He slept nude under the duvet after a long soak in the bath. The vet's painkillers ensured he slept well enough, and he woke, stiff, to wintry sunshine and a crust of snow on the deep-set window. The pub had no central heating and the fire of the evening before had long since gone out.

He was reluctant to get up to put on his stained clothes and he needed some time to think now that his head felt clearer. Why had those men broken into the car, tried to stop him on the road and what connection did those incidents have with the intruder at his office?

He tried to remember what they looked like but he only had a general impression from the few seconds the two cars had been close together. He had a vague idea of their build and their ages from where he'd seen them at a distance in Biggar, but his full attention then had been on David.

The man in the passenger seat of the car was probably the one who had pushed David to the ground and he was also the heavier of the two. He might recognize him again. He could have died in that gully—if the farm worker had not seen him go over the edge—and yet the men in the car had done nothing to help. They hadn't reported what had happened. What sort of people were they, for Christ's sake?

He threw back the duvet and jumped out of bed, went to the window and saw that the landscape was white. The branches of the fir trees were weighed down with snow, and there wasn't a bird to be seen, nor a farm animal. He shivered and discovered that Betty had laid out some of her son's clothes for him. Tim was not as tall as he was, so the cords were short and he tucked them into the rugby socks. The Aran jumper was better, but there were no shoes. He went downstairs when he smelled bacon frying, and met Betty's husband, Joe, whom he had not met the night before.

'I've got a suitcase in the car,' he said after a good break-fast, but Joe shook his head.

'You'll not get that back until they fetch up the car. I'll see to that if you like.'

'Still, I'd like to walk along there, to have a look at the place in daylight,' John said. 'It's hard to believe it happened, so I want to see just what the drop is like.' That sounded morbid but Joe seemed to understand.

'They were going to put up a better fence, maybe now they will,' he said. 'It's a bad corner if you don't know the road.'

They found a pair of wellingtons that fitted him and an anorak belonging to Joe, and John trudged along the road with his hands in his pockets. The small hamlet had a row of cottages, a post-office-cum-store and a garage that no doubt serviced the farm machinery. A hundred yards further on he was on the long bend and it was easy to spot where his car had gone over because of the new gashes on the tree-trunks.

Fresh snow had almost covered the tracks on the grass verge but he saw that his footprints were not the only ones that were fresh. A car had stopped there recently and some-one had walked to the same place. Inspector Jamieson no doubt had stopped there on his way to work, to inspect the spot in daylight. John held on to the trunk of a tree and leaned out to look down on his car. The vet's description had been right; his car was hooked by the branch that went right through the windscreen and the tree itself was on the edge of a sheer drop. It was a sturdy old tree but landslips had taken the soil from its roots and now the main trunk was leaning out over the river.

There were deep grooves in the thick leaf mould showing where the car had gone down and where his rescuers had struggled to get him and themselves back up the slope, but it occurred to John that those marks might hide the traces of someone else having been down there later. It was a suggestion he couldn't brush off as far-fetched, either, because the men had been so determined to make him stop, but what they'd hoped to find was beyond him.

The open boot of his car was facing him and there was no sign of his suitcase in it and Joe would have told him if it had been brought up—but on the other hand it could have sprung open during the car's descent and the case could now be in the river . . .

It was Tollis who came in the green Range-Rover to collect him and John was relieved that Rees hadn't come in person. Tollis might not have a lot to say, but he was a restful person to be with and wouldn't press him to discuss what had happened.

'You all right?' was all he said after John had said good-bye to Betty and Joe.

He glanced over John's odd assortment of clothes and the dressing on his forehead and then reached to start the engine. 'It will be the first time the girls in reception have let anyone like you inside the building.' And for Tollis that was humour.

'They won't see me like this. I'll change at the flat first.'

Tollis shook his head. 'Rees wants to see you right away.'

'It won't take long, and I can't go around like this,' John protested, lifting a green wellington to prove his point. Tollis said nothing for a bit and seemed to be concentrating on his driving, but at last he looked over at John.

'You can't go to your flat. Rees sent somebody there to get you fresh clothes this morning and he found the door open. It's a mess. Everything is smashed all to hell.'

John felt a sickening lurch deep in his abdomen. 'I don't believe this.'

'Look, we'll go to see Rees and talk it all out. There's no point in saying anything until we're all sitting down together.'

'After I've been to the flat.' John made it clear that he wasn't prepared to argue on that point. 'Just take me there first so that I can see it for myself.'

'The police may be there still,' Tollis pointed out, but he drove on in silence until they reached the city outskirts where dirty snow was piled high in the gutters. He still hadn't spoken when he turned off and headed for Stockbridge.

And during that time John was thinking of the flat, how he hardly used it these days except as somewhere to sleep. He and Trish had bought it when they married and he'd changed nothing after she was killed.

He had thought of moving several times but he'd never got around to actually doing it. It would have been too final. In the beginning it would have meant admitting that she was gone for good and later he'd been loath to shut the door on the memories. There had been nothing to motivate him into looking for somewhere else.

Tollis stopped in the main street and looked with raised eyebrows at John.

'No, I'll go up on my own,' John said.

There was only one policeman still there and he was about to seal the door. John told him who he was and the man agreed to let him look around. 'We've done all we want anyway,' he said.

He stayed in the close as John stepped warily inside, afraid of what he'd find and the first thing was broken glass under his feet. Then a sour smell filled his nose and he tracked that down to his bedroom where all his clothes had been removed from the wardrobe and dumped on the floor. The bedlinen was piled on top and it was from this heap that the smell came. He moved closer and then was repelled when he realized that someone had sprayed urine over everything. In all the other rooms the surfaces had been swept clear, curtains pulled down, pictures removed from the walls. It was all smashed, trampled under feet that had delighted in wrecking his home. Photographs were scattered around and he salvaged a few that had escaped being fouled by urine.

Nothing else was worth saving. It hadn't been expensively furnished. Most of the bits and pieces didn't even match because in those early days of marriage they had bought what they could afford. They went to auctions and he had a sudden vivid picture of Trish's delight when she had the highest bid. She didn't know the finer points of bidding and instead of a discreet nod she waved her brochure. The auctioneer and regular dealers had got to know her and because her excitement was so infectious they soon called her by name. One or two even kept their eyes open for things she wanted and they would phone up and tell her about a nice coffee table or a picture they'd seen. And she'd be off, slender as a boy in tight jeans, her fair hair tied back from her face, aglow with excitement.

The memories were very vivid and the old pains of grief were awakened. John kicked aside slashed cushions from the suite and uncovered a picture that had been a favourite. Somehow it had escaped damage and he picked it up. Two horses in a field full of buttercups. Trish had chosen it because she said the horses were in love. 'Just look at the way he's nuzzling her neck.'

'Like this?' he'd said, brushing his lips against the back of her neck. Any excuse to make love . . .

Since entering the flat he'd felt anger rising in his chest and now it exploded. 'Damn you!' he shouted at the bare windows. 'Bastards!'

The word trailed away as he surveyed the room. He couldn't believe what he was seeing. The last remnants of his marriage were gone, smashed and fouled.

The policeman came silently into the room and stood just inside the door. He seemed willing to wait patiently but John had had enough. He turned to face him, wanting some hint that the men who had done this would be found and gaoled.

'What sort of animals are they?' he asked savagely, and although the policeman had probably seen it all before he still showed sympathy.

'If they don't find anything worth taking and if they have the time . . . they like to do this. Don't ask me why,' he added in disgust. 'They weren't pros anyway. A pro wouldn't have smashed the lock to get in. Wonder why your neighbours didn't hear anything?'

'In this area people go into their flats and shut out the world. I don't know many of them even by sight,' John said wearily. He followed the policeman out and pulled the outer door shut and while his hand was still on the doorknob, he said goodbye to the flat and his wife. He knew he would never come back. It was finished. The animals who had taken such delight in smashing his home and finally made him say goodbye to his Trish and he wanted to face them one day. He wanted to drive his fists into their faces and he felt no shock at the violence of his feelings.

He wanted to find them and make them suffer and the feeling wasn't going to go away.

Tollis said nothing as he drove across the centre of town,

up the Mound, and past the Castle that looked even bleaker with snow lying on the gashes of bare rock below it. The heavy grey sky seemed to rest on the very walls of the castle and it was as if the same cold stone was in the centre of John's chest. Then they were pulling into the back of the Kramer building and his thoughts were a jumble of images and his head throbbed with an ache that was purely emotional. He followed Tollis through the entrance hall, where receptionists were trained to stop anyone proceeding further without an appointment. The girls stared at the grim faces of the two men who strode to the stairs, took in John's weird assortment of clothes, guessed that something terrible had happened.

'He saw the flat,' Tollis told Rees as soon as they entered Rees's office. Then he glanced at his watch. 'I've got an hour, so we can't waste time if we want to hear what John has to say.'

'Any news?' Rees was obviously referring to something to do with Sentinel because Tollis merely shook his head and Rees seemed to understand.

'I'd like to say something first,' John said. 'I met a policeman in Altford. A Chief Inspector Robert Jamieson.'

He looked directly at Rees as he spoke and saw the muscles of Rees's face tighten with irritation? Anger?

'He hinted—no, he made a point of telling me—that the people who work for Rees are often involved in "accidents". I want to know what he meant. It struck me on the way up here that if he thinks that way, there may be other people who think that I work for you, or for Tollis.' The anger he'd been bottling up since he saw his home wrecked now made his voice too loud, too abrupt, and it was all aimed at Rees, his uncle.

But Tollis was nodding in agreement. 'We've had the same thought, but there's more to it than that. It's fairly obvious to me that you've got something that someone else wants.'

'That's nonsense. And who is this "someone"?'

Tollis shrugged and for once his laid-back attitude irritated John. 'That's for you to tell us. Since that intruder at your office, things have escalated. So start at the beginning —with that first incident. Is there anything in your office that's new, some document or piece of information about one of your clients . . . anything that someone else would risk all this for?

'Nothing. The usual files, pages of figures . . . I don't even have a typewriter or a spare suit there. And there's something else that you don't know about yet. Two men followed me to Biggar and tried to break into my car yesterday morning.'

'So they decided to see if you had it with you, what ever "it" is, and they followed you to Biggar and kept an eye on you over the weekend. Did you get the number of the other car—the one that presumably hung around until you left Gwen's and then followed you?'

'No, they ran off—it all happened very quickly. And I've tried to remember what they looked like. One was almost my height, about mid-thirties, scruffy, dark straggling hair —touching his collar and unwashed. He was the one I saw closest. The other one was smaller. He stayed back, I didn't take much notice of him. The car was a grey BMW—it did seem strange that men like that would drive such an expensive car.'

'Close your eyes, John, and try to see it and the men. Did it have any markings, mascots hanging in the window, dents?'

John did as Tollis asked and let the sequence when the other car was alongside him run like a film. He could see the other man's face, his angry gestures. 'The bigger man had a broken nose—there wasn't anything special about the car.'

'OK. Now go through it all, from the time you saw them at you car outside Gwen's. Don't push it, let it come as you saw it.'

Tollis made it sound easy, but John did as he was asked, told them from the time that David ran ahead, and as he pictured the man brush David aside, he saw what the man was wearing. Jeans and dirty trainers.

'So it could be the same man that was in your office, but lots of people wear jeans and trainers—you do.'

Rees was saying nothing, just listening intently, but John could see that he was agitated. So he continued with the rest, right up to the point where he was pulled up the slope by the men from Altford.

'And it's possible that someone may have gone down into that gully to take my suitcase. I went along there to see the place for myself and the case wasn't in the boot, but I suppose it could have fallen out if the boot burst open in the fall, and they would have one hell of a struggle to negotiate that slope in the dark.'

Tollis had taken notes and he wrote that down too. 'I forgot that Jamieson was living in Altford now so he'll soon hear about your flat and then he'll link the two things up. And he'll come to the same conclusion as Rees and I. You have something that someone else wants and we have to find out what it is before they try for it again.'

He stretched and then rubbed his eyes and John noticed for the first time that Tollis looked as if he'd been up all night.

He was always immaculately dressed when interviewing clients or out on a job, but his inclination was to dress for comfort. Now, his coat was so crumpled that he looked as if he'd slept all night in a draughty doorway, but perhaps he had. The man was so reticent that he could even sleep in his office for all anyone knew.

John was getting tired of protesting that he had nothing of interest to anyone else, but Tollis insisted that he now went through everything that he'd taken with him to Gwen's for the weekend.

'Start with packing your case. Picture it and you'll remember better. Then think of loading the car—you took one from the pool, didn't you, so we don't have to worry about the glove compartment.'

John listed his clothes, the gift-wrapped camera and films that were for David's birthday. He'd taken his own camera but there was no spool in it until he put in a fresh one when he got there. 'And I took a couple of spares. There was my briefcase with Rees's files in it—no one would be interested in them, would they?'

Tollis looked to Rees, who shrugged. 'Survey reports, mostly. I've got copies and so have the clients.'

'And I took a couple of paperbacks and some of those sweets that Gwen likes.'

'You're absolutely sure there was nothing else?'

'I'm certain.'

'Then it may have been something you had on you, in your wallet? It wasn't in your flat or they wouldn't have stayed to wreck it.'

John emptied the pockets of his borrowed cords. 'These came from the pockets of my jeans. The rest of my stuff is still in the car, my sheepskin was on the back seat, the case in the boot.' He pulled everything out of his wallet and Tollis poked through it all and then sighed.

'There's only one more place,' he said, not meeting John's eyes. 'Clare's flat.'

It took a moment for that to sink in and then the implication hit John. He stood up and reached for the phone, but Tollis stopped him. 'Don't tell her yet, John.'

John ignored him and dialled Clare's office number. While he waited for her to answer he spoke angrily to Tollis. 'What if they broke into her flat when she was there . . . have you thought of that?'

'This has all blown up in a matter of days. If you haven't seen her for a week, say, they won't know that she exists.' Tollis still spoke in a reasoning tone.

'So I'll just make sure,' John said.

Clare was pleased he'd phoned. As usual, he felt better just for hearing her voice and it was obvious that no one had been bothering her. She was the only really sane person in his life at the moment, beautiful pragmatic Clare.

'I just wanted to let you know I'm back and that I'll call you later.'

'You haven't forgotten I'm going on a course on Thursday, have you? A short one, three days—back Sunday.' He had forgotten. The details seemed part of another life.

'She's all right,' he said as he hung up. 'So where do we go from here?'

John knew now how it felt to be accused of a crime, to be involved in a case of mistaken identity. He couldn't protest to these faceless people that they had the wrong man because he didn't know who to protest to.

'We wait and see what happens next and in the meantime my men will make inquiries about the car.'

'And I'm the tethered goat? I'll be looking over my shoulder all the time.'

Tollis looked right back at him without speaking and John knew that the man was saying there was nothing else they could do.

'I don't believe this—why can't we just tell the police what's been going on?' He saw Tollis look sharply at Rees.

'There's no reason, none at all,' Tollis said. 'But I don't think you'll have to go to them, they'll be coming to you.

In the meantime maybe Mike could stay with you. He's at a loose end and you'd be doing him a favour . . .'

'No. I need time to think and I don't want a babysitter.'

And John strode out of Rees's office to do the only thing that made sense—he went to buy himself some new clothes.

CHAPTER 6

He bought a couple of off-the-peg suits and some casual clothes, changed into one set and had the shop wrap those lent to him by Betty. Princes Street was crowded but that didn't make him feel safe because watching eyes could belong to anyone in the crowd—who might even be at his shoulder. In Boots he bought a razor since his was still in his suitcase and he might never see that again.

He had walked down from Kramer's and now he went back there but didn't go to Rees's office. Instead he asked one of the girls to look after his parcels and told her that he was taking a car. 'If my uncle asks, I'll be back this afternoon sometime.'

He wanted to get away from people, so he picked up a pack of sandwiches from a takeaway and then drove down to the Granton yacht harbour to eat them. He sat in the car on the quayside for a long time, looking at the yachts, some of which were laid up for the winter and were covered in tarpaulins.

He remembered childhood trips with his parents from this small harbour and wondered if they had ever realized how frightened he'd been each time they hit the choppy waters of the Forth. He never did enjoy sailing.

As far as he was able to tell, no one had followed him. No cars were parked within sight and the quay was deserted. The sea was as grey as the sky and overhead gulls were using the air currents to hover and soar and their mournful calls seemed to match the way he was feeling.

He was scared and it was a new feeling. He was mixed up in something that was straight out of a second-rate film and he had no background to deal with it. He was an accountant and while he was bored with it, he was still the sort of person who enjoyed pages of figures and the logic that went with them. They were equations that followed a set pattern and always ended up as predicted.

How could he fight something he didn't understand? And Rees, the man who had always seemed so strong, now seemed incapable of advising him. Only Tollis had any purpose and he was busy with his own Agency's affairs.

He tried to plan what he should do. His office had to function but there was nothing there that couldn't wait for a day or so. He had to see Clare, which would be difficult to arrange without telling her what was going on and he couldn't put her in danger by going to her place.

He was damned if he was going to have Mike Cairns tagging along with him as a bodyguard. No doubt the police in the form of Chief Inspector Jamieson would soon be asking questions . . . which Rees—for reasons of his own —would hate. Well that was too bad, but he, John Leith, was no part of Kramer's or Sentinel, and he had no intention of playing Rees's secret games nor was he going to play hide-and-seek with whoever was searching his belongings.

Let them come out into the open. He felt better for having that sorted out in his mind. He drove back to Kramer House, parked the car and found Rees still in his office. He had swung his chair around to face the window and seemed so lost in thought that he didn't hear John enter.

It was very quiet in that room. The double-glazing cut the traffic sounds down to a murmur and thick carpeting insulated the room from other office sounds. Just along the corridor girls were working, laughing, and yet in Rees's room he could hear nothing. It was a tidy room in contrast to Tollis's which hummed with activity. The large desk under the window was clear of files, the coffee table had a squared-off stack of property brochures piled on its polished surface. And it was gloomy because Rees had let the blinds fall to half-way and he was now a hunched shadow in the depths of his chair. He hadn't moved since John entered the room.

'Rees? Are you all right?'

His uncle jerked and then turned and in the instant before he smiled, John saw the utter depression in his eyes. 'Yes,' he said briskly. 'It's a sign of old age that I spend time in thinking instead of doing. Where did you get to?'

'Granton, at the harbour. I just needed some space. Why don't you go home and let Janet spoil you for a bit? This place can run itself now.'

'I was thinking of doing that. And you could use the flat upstairs until yours is cleaned up.'

John hadn't even thought about where he was to sleep that night and it solved an immediate problem. Clare could come there in safety too, which solved another.

'Thanks.' He hesitated because he'd intended to ask his uncle some questions and now he wasn't sure that Rees was fit to be asked anything. His uncle looked preoccupied and haggard.

'If Mike is still at a loose end maybe he'll drive you down to Elmwood,' he suggested quietly. 'I could hang about here and maybe grab something to eat with Tollis this evening—I'll stick around anyway and keep an eye on things.' And to his relief Rees seemed ready to fall in with anything he said, except he refused point blank to have Mike as driver, so he phoned down to Tollis and told him what Rees was going to do.

'That's what I was hoping—his housekeeper will look after him and he's better out of here for the moment,' Tollis said. 'When he's gone, I'd like a word with you.'

John agreed to that because then Tollis could answer his questions. As soon as he saw Rees away, he phoned Clare.

'Sorry I cut you off before,' he said. 'I was with Rees and Tollis.'

'You were supposed to call last night.' No reproof, just a statement. 'Are we eating out tonight?'

'No, but I'll cook you breakfast if you like.' He heard her giggle. 'Look, there are a lot of things happening right now and I need to talk to you but you'll have to come here—Kramer House. I know it sounds crazy but . . .'

'Is something wrong? You sound so mysterious.'

'I'll explain when I see you. Come along when you can, but I don't suppose Rees keeps much food in the flat so you'd better grab a snack somewhere first.'

'You're joking.' She sounded amused and curious.

'No, I'm not. Will you come?'

'All right, but you'd better have a good story ready.'

After he'd hung up he sat for a while behind his uncle's desk. He was Rees's heir and he knew that Rees expected him to take over the business one day but it had always been a decision that he would face sometime in the future. But if Rees was thinking about full retirement—which might be the reason for his preoccupation—that day might come sooner than he'd thought. And he wasn't sure he wanted to be in Rees's shoes, yet.

He told Rees's secretary that his uncle was taking a few days off and then used the stairs down to the Sentinel floor.

'I'm glad you talked Rees into going home,' Tollis said, and as if he had read John's thoughts he went on, 'And I think you should take it a step further; lock up your office and bring your stuff to Kramer's and use one of the spare rooms. After all, you won't have Tracy to help out, and apart from being more secure, it makes sense.'

John agreed. 'And I'll see if someone could act as manager for Rees—I know he wants me to take over in the long term but I don't see myself in the property business.'

Tollis grinned. 'I thought you might say that.'

John was impatient to leave the subject alone. 'I can't concentrate on selling houses with all this going on. I want to know what that policeman meant when he said that Rees's employees often have accidents. From the way he said it he meant that they knew their job was dangerous. Is it, and why was Rees so reluctant to tell Jamieson anything?'

'Last part first. Rees can't change habits—secrets and intrigue—he wants to do everything for himself. You don't really know him, do you? And Jamieson won't believe that Rees no longer has anything to do with Sentinel. Kramer House, to Jamieson, means Rees Kramer—a lot of clients still think he runs all of it.' Tollis settled in his chair and studied John, as if assessing how much he should tell him. 'I've hit a quiet spell for the first time today so you might as well be told something about what we do here. Yes, working in a security firm can be dangerous but mostly the work is routine and extremely boring. Firstly, we are investigators, and nowadays that doesn't mean snooping on wandering husbands as much as it used to. We do a lot of paperwork, following up leads that anyone could do, only we know how to do it better. We often get called in by firms who suspect industrial espionage; we look for planted bugs or a director on the take or a cleaner who goes through waste-paper bins for scraps of information when a take-over is planned.

'Then there's the other side, the routine security set-ups, guards and dogs.' He waved a hand to illustrate that the list was a long one. 'We charge a lot of money for the intensive investigations but the firms are at risk of losing millions in some cases, so they pay. But when large sums of money are involved, there can be danger. We don't break the law, despite what Jamieson thinks, because there is no need. We have a good reputation and all our men are well trained, but the trouble is that anyone can set up a firm like this and some of them are cowboys.

'Policemen like Jamieson don't like the cowboys, natur-

ally, and some of their suspicions reflect back on us. I don't
like it, but the best way to win them over is to cooperate.
Rees was always reluctant to do that for some deep reason
all his own.' Tollis shrugged, as if he had little understand-
ing of Rees's motives.

'Jamieson made it sound as if he and Rees were enemies.'

Tollis agreed. 'He's a good policeman and he doesn't
like private companies doing anything that resembles police
work. Do you know about how we got started? Rees and I
were in the army together, in military intelligence, and that
gave us the experience to start this business but when we
got successful, some of those who were still in the service
thought we could do the odd job for them.' He paused while
John absorbed that.

'What sort of jobs?'

Tollis spread his hands eloquently. 'We're larger than
most of this sort of firm—we have a lot branches and a lot
of employees. Our men are ex-forces or from the police
force, all highly trained men, and we have the spread of
resources that Special Branch doesn't have. If we could
help in any way we did, but that was Rees's doing—I can't
say I was ever keen to get involved and nowadays I do my
best to keep well away from that kind of . . . extra contract
work. Jamieson knows and resents what he calls "interference in police work". And he's right.'

John felt a shiver run down his spine, like iced water that
touched each vertebra in turn.

'Are you doing anything like that right now?'

Tollis looked solemn. 'Not really. Well, Rees seems to
have instigated something off his own bat, but it wasn't a
big job.' He looked very uncomfortable, and when Tollis
revealed anything of what he was feeling John knew that
something was happening. 'There's no point in going into
that now and I've decided that in future there won't be any
more of it. Rees knew how I felt about it a long time ago.

We almost broke up the partnership because we disagreed about it all the time and that's when I took sole charge of Sentinel.'

'Rees wouldn't have reported the break-in in at my flat either, would he?'

Tollis shrugged. 'He didn't get the chance. That was the man he sent to fetch your clothes. Rees hates police involvement in what he thinks is no one's business but our own and lately . . . well, I think it's time he got out altogether.' Abruptly, Tollis ended that conversation. 'Now, let's go and eat before anyone discovers I've nothing to do,' he went on. And over a pizza he asked John if he would at least keep an eye on the Kramer work for a while. 'It would please Rees, and it will keep him out of my hair.'

Tollis had eaten his food mechanically, as if it was merely a fuel that his body needed and now he was fidgeting to get back to work. He paid the bill, gathered up his creased raincoat and moved purposefully to the door. 'It was a good idea to let you stay in Rees's flat. I won't be going home tonight—I've got a bed of sorts in my back room. So if you feel like some company . . . ?'

'Clare's coming over. I thought if she came in while the staff was still around, no one would guess who she was.'

'So there's no point in expecting you later?'

'Mm, probably not.' John grinned.

'I expect you've heard it many times before, but shouldn't you marry that girl before someone else does?'

'She won't have me,' John said.

Which was only half true because he'd never actually proposed to her, but from things she'd said about friends who were married, he knew that it wasn't something she was anxious to enter into herself. And since he'd felt the same way, they'd drifted comfortably along, probably happier than they would have been if the knot had been legally tied. It worked. She was twenty-nine, a woman who knew exactly where she was going in her career as a senior civil servant. She was fun to be with and they were good in bed but there was a lot more than that, although he was damned if he could put it into words. They matched, that was all. They just didn't bother to analyse it.

'Then I'll assume that you're not alone, but feel free to join me for a drink if you are,' Tollis said as they parted.

And from Rees's office John phoned down to ask the porter to let him know when Clare arrived. While he waited he looked out Rees's copies of the files he'd taken to Biggar, which presumably were now lost. He'd already glanced through them at Gwen's and now he saw that his memory of what they contained was accurate enough. Survey reports of proposed land sales, samples of the publicity, and in some cases a few loose ends to be tied up. As Rees had said, the clients had copies and there was nothing at all in the folders that could possibly interest a third party. No secret developments to interest speculators, nothing. As Tollis had pointed out, they couldn't do much until something else developed and that meant he was the tethered goat and there was nothing he could do until the other side sent in the tiger.

CHAPTER 7

Clare Aitken had dark glossy hair that hung loose on her shoulders. The cold wind had tossed strands across her face and she brushed them away as she dropped her briefcase in the sitting-room of the small flat.

She took one look at the bruises and stitches on his face and walked straight into his arms. 'Were you in an accident?' And for the first time in days John felt the tension ease out of his body.

'Sort of,' he said.

She had brought the night air in with her and her skin glowed with freshness. She was still in her office clothes, an executive-style black suit, but the skirt was long and flowing and a raspberry silk blouse sent reflections of colour up on to her cheeks, taking away the formality of it. She looked good enough to eat and suddenly he wanted to take her to bed.

As usual, she knew exactly what he was thinking but she wanted an explanation first.

Hooking her fingers into his sweater, she shook him in mock indignation. 'Not now.' She was torn between laughter and concern. 'Tell me what happened.'

So he told her everything, sitting beside her with his arm loosely around her shoulders. He kept to the bald facts, without any of the conclusions reached by Tollis and Rees and she listened intently, although once or twice it seemed that she wanted to interrupt him.

He was interested in what her reactions would be because Tollis and Rees had a knowledge of crime, while Clare was his equal, a level-headed young woman; she was ignorant of anything to do with the criminal world.

'You should have been honest with the police right from the start,' she said firmly.

'With hindsight, I agree completely, but I was trusting Rees's advice at the time. Anyway, that policeman I met at Altford will be looking me up and then I'll have to come clean.'

'They have records—maybe they'll know the likely people to question and then you wouldn't need to hide out in this flat.' She looked around angrily but he knew her anger wasn't directed at him. It was the helpless sort of emotion that he'd been holding in for days because it had no outlet.

'Oh . . .' She let out a long sigh and leaned against him so that her hair spread out on his chest.

He dropped his chin on to the top of her head and knew that even in silence they understood each other perfectly.

'It's changed you,' she said and her words were muffled, so he lifted her chin up so that he could see her face. Her dark lashes were like smudges on the cool clear skin and there was a question in her eyes. To stop it he bent to kiss her.

'It has,' she insisted and the kiss became a hit and miss collision of lips and teeth and he tasted her lipstick. He was impatient for the bedroom now but Clare would have her say. A good civil servant, she spent her life dealing in facts, whittling away the trivia and making decisions on what was left. Now she was applying that skill to his problems.

'This isn't your scene, John—you're not the sort to play detective, but under the worry I sense a bit of enjoyment of the puzzle.'

True. There was an excitement that was new and it was adding a zing to his life, but given a choice it wouldn't have been such a dangerous one. 'I'm just beginning to realize that I don't know *what* type I am,' he admitted ruefully. 'I seem to have been asleep for a long time.'

'But it's serious!' She sat up. 'These men are really dangerous.'

'Mm.'

She snuggled against him again and stretched one arm around his waist to pull herself even closer. 'Like shadow-boxing, only they can see the target.'

Bang on the button, he thought. He'd wondered how to approach the danger of the situation without frightening her, but she was working it out for herself and as he'd expected, she was calm and logical.

'So you don't want to be seen with me in case . . .'

'That's right,' he said quickly. 'The police can't provide bodyguards but if there's no connection between you and me you'll be perfectly safe.'

'I feel safe now,' she said softly. 'I've never seen you like this. You're usually so . . . laid-back.'

'Prostrate,' he agreed with a grin. 'And speaking of lying down . . .'

In the bedroom they dropped their clothes and let them lie on the floor. It was a long time since either of them had felt such urgency in their love-making and it was as if danger added spice to their coming together. They were simply two people who knew each other's needs, who knew each other's bodies as well as their own, with the desire to share an old, old pleasure. In the end it was with love and not just to satisfy a need. It hadn't ever been quite like that before.

They lay in silence for a long time afterwards, bodies clammy and relaxed with pleasured exhaustion. And it was as if each knew what the other was thinking, that tonight they would come together again and again to see if this extreme pleasure would last. Clare's hair was tumbled as she lay smiling and naked in his arms on the tossed bed-clothes and uneasily he wondered if it would all end when he told her about David coming to live with him.

'Clare.' Now was as good a time as any, before the morning took him back to reality. 'Gwen's going to move to Aberdeen and I have to make a decision about my son.' She lay still and then brushed her hair back from her face.

'I knew you'd have to one day,' she said quietly. 'Does it matter?'

'No, not in the least. I just wanted you to know what I'd decided. I'll buy a house and make a new start but I have to know how you feel.'

'About marriage? In the future maybe, but I like what we already have—let's see how it works out.' She leaned across him and kissed him gently and he felt a muscle ripple across her abdomen as if she was experiencing a private climax. All thoughts of the future were put firmly in their place.

In the Sentinel office, Tollis assessed the information that had been coming in concerning Toby Cairns. Most of it consisted of rumours or guesswork from contacts who hoped to get some reward from the Kramer organization.

Toby had vanished and the only conclusion he came to was that Toby was either being held somewhere, or he was dead. Mike was already insisting that the police be called in, but there wouldn't be much that the police could do because Toby was an adult who could disappear if he chose to and there was no evidence that anything violent had happened to him. And Albert Gumley was not likely to notify anyone that was missing. Sighing, Tollis reached for the phone and asked if Chief Inspector Jamieson was available.

And while he waited, he knew that if all else failed, he would ask John to approach Gumley because he was the only one certain of getting into the house and probably that was what would have to happen in the end.

'Jamieson here,' a deep voice said in his ear. 'What can I do for you? Is your Mr Leith in more hot water?'

'I think we'd better talk about that and another matter,' Tollis said.

'Can it wait until morning? I'm involved in something at the moment.'

Tollis agreed that it could, and after he hung up he was tempted by the thought of the camp-bed in his back room but instead poured himself another cup of strong black coffee.

He wondered if Clare Aitken had stayed the night . . . and if John would marry her eventually. She was right for him if only he would let go of past memories. He never spoke of his wife or the circumstances of her death and it was likely that Clare had no idea of the effects that trau-matic time had had on him. Maybe she'd be the catalyst, make John speak about it and do what no one else had been able to do: make him accept that his wife was gone and was never coming back.

It would be better for everyone, especially Rees, who had banked everything on the prospect of John taking over the business one day. But in the meantime there was Toby Cairns and Albert Gumley, and Tollis rubbed the back of his hand over eyes that felt as if they were full of grit. Lack of sleep never bothered him. He catnapped, a minute here and a minute there, even sitting at his desk he could shut his eyes and sleep at odd moments. And he was getting too old for it, was doubtful of his own judgement at times.

The Sentinel Agency had taken over too much of his life and yet it was all he had. No wife, no real home. He yawned and once more went over the reports that his men had brought in. Where was Toby Cairns?

CHAPTER 8

Clare left shortly before 7.30 in the morning because she had to get back to her flat to change for work. She was outwardly cheerful, bright-eyed and beautiful, with no hint that she'd had little sleep. She seemed to be looking forward to her flight the next day—or so she would have him believe. Only when he went with her down through the silent office block and kissed her goodbye did she reveal what she was really thinking about.

'Take care,' she said simply.

'I will. Let me know your flight back and I'll pick you up at Turnhouse on Sunday.'

On the way back upstairs he dropped in on Tollis who looked as if he'd been up most of the night as usual. 'One of the girls brings me in hot bacon rolls. Stay if you like,' he said, yawning hugely. He was still wearing yesterday's shirt and the air in his room was stale.

'Did Rees phone you last night?' He shaved as he talked and yet another cigarette burned away in an ashtray.

'No, and I'm not calling him in case he feels like coming back,' John said. 'He looked done in yesterday.'

'That may be my fault. We had words and he was warned last year to take things easy after a sort of angina thing.' He tossed the razor in the direction of his desk where it dislodged a pile of files which slithered across papers he'd been working on, and John wondered briefly how Tollis functioned in such chaos.

'I've a favour to ask you,' Tollis said briskly, as if by shaving off his stubble he was now fresh and ready for action. 'You may not like it, though.'

'I've nothing planned for today except ducking my shadows,' John said lightly.

'That's what I thought. Well, this has nothing to do with any of that—it's purely a Sentinel job. A young man who had just started working here has gone missing and you could get some information for me—in fact you're probably the only person who can.'

'I'm intrigued.'

'Wait to hear the rest before you agree,' Tollis warned. 'Rees got one of his vague requests for help from the Special Branch. They wanted us to keep an eye on your father-in-law.'

Albert Gumley again. John felt like calling a halt to it right then, but at that moment the girl arrived with the bacon rolls in polystyrene boxes and as they ate, John let his curiosity over-ride his dislike of Gumley.

Tollis explained. 'Rees didn't discuss it with me for obvious reasons, I would have refused. So he simply got hold of young Toby and sent him on the job.'

'How does it work—this request from the police?'

'Very casually, nothing on paper. A quiet word in a pub and it's never official. In this case there was a flood of drugs about and the spotlight fell on Gumley for some reason. So Rees sent Toby along to watch the comings and goings.'

'Drugs?'

Tollis nodded when he saw John's sceptical expression. 'Exactly what I thought. It's crazy.'

'And Toby disappeared.'

'Not a word since Thursday. Rees didn't think there would be any danger and I have to admit I agree with him there—I'd never believe Gumley dangerous. The man's on his last gasp, after all, but Rees still had no business sending an untrained man on any job at all. Dammit, he left Sentinel to me but he won't stay out of it!'

'That's why he was so depressed, then.'

'I'm afraid I didn't pull any punches.' Tollis seemed to be reliving the angry scene he'd had with Rees as he prowled the room. 'He was in the wrong and I told him so.'

'And you think Gumley will tell me what happened to the man? Not a chance. For one thing he hates my guts and he wouldn't tell me a thing.'

'I wonder.' Tollis stopped pacing. 'He takes a great interest in Kramer's and in you—he phones Rees just to let him know that he's keeping in touch with what goes on.'

'I didn't know that.' But it was just the sort of thing the man *would* do. 'He's never forgiven me for fighting him over custody of David. He hadn't a hope of winning and he knew it, but he enjoyed putting pressure on me. I use it against him, though. I threaten to stop the visits if he interferes in any way and the friction just keeps on and on. It's not as if he was a real father to Trish—she never saw him after her mother walked out on him—but it might have been different if he'd had a son. What is it with men like that? They want their seed carried on, an heir to carry the name . . . Why didn't Rees ever mention that Gumley phoned him?'

'Need to know. It didn't rub off Rees, the old rule about keeping your mouth shut unless you had to pass information along.' Tollis shook his head. 'Rees should have stayed in the army. I know for certain that Gumley was in touch with him recently because I caught the tail end of the conversation and you'd have thought I was spying on a state secret.'

What could Rees and Gumley have to talk about, John wondered? The fact that he wore jeans to work? That he only took on enough clients to pay the rent? Was Gumley really interested in him? Then another thought occurred.

'Rees sent Toby to Gumley's and the day after he went missing, a man hit me over the head.'

The words hung in the air for a few seconds only before Tollis shook his head. 'I can't see it. Gumley would have no reason, unless . . . Did he blame you for his daughter's death? A sick old man could be eaten up with hatred festering away inside him.'

'I never found out what he felt. He turned up at the funeral but we had no contact until he decided he wanted David. You were around then, so you know.'

Tollis fiddled with the papers on his desk. 'Rees asked me to help and I knew that a bottle wasn't your answer.'

And the memories came surging back. Rees coming to tell him that a drunk had lost control of his car and had driven up on to the pavement where Trish was pushing the pram. Rees hadn't known any other way of breaking the news except by a bald statement of the facts and it had been Tollis who came later to take away the booze.

Tollis told him that Gwen was looking after David. He hadn't cared. A baby of four weeks had no personality, didn't even smile, and was too new in his life to have any meaning when Trish had been wrenched from it. Witnesses at the inquest said that she pushed the pram clear before the car hit her. She had cared.

'I don't know if he blames me but I felt guilty at the time. If I'd been there . . . I kept telling myself it would never have happened if I'd been there.' He hadn't put that into words before and he still couldn't speak about the nightmares. Night after night he'd seen her accident so vividly described at the inquest and each night Trish was again tossed into the air, her long fair hair swirling out like a shawl. In his dreams he tried to break her fall but his outstretched arms never managed to catch her.

'Fighting him over David was a help,' he admitted evenly. 'Christ, I've wasted a lot of time with my son and having Gumley around my neck doesn't help. If I'm a day late taking David to visit him he's on the phone. Yes, I think he would do me harm but not if it meant losing touch with his grandson. He's an evil old bugger but David genuinely likes him—maybe no one else ever has.'

'He has the men. There are a lot of old cronies around him in that house—as far as I know no woman has set foot in it—and they're loyal. But would a dying old man who's made his pile suddenly start dealing in drugs when he wouldn't touch them in the past? It doesn't ring true.'

John shrugged. As far as he was concerned, Gumley was capable of anything.

'By the way, I kept track of that drunk driver.' Tollis wanted to round off that particular episode now that John had discussed it. 'He took his family off to Australia when he got out of prison and his liver finally conked out. He died there.'

Once, John would have relished that news but now he felt nothing at all. No anger, no remorse for the man's family. It had happened seven years ago and the grief had left him numb—it might have happened to someone else.

'All right, I'll go and see Gumley, but what reason do I give? I'm not due to take David until Christmas.'

Tollis tapped the desk with a pen, looking pensive, and then he laughed. 'Knowing him, I'd say he probably knows exactly what's been going on with you—why not be honest and ask him who's behind it? Then you could slip in a question about Toby.'

John liked the idea. 'When do I go?'

'As soon as possible. I'm at a dead end and this morning Jamieson will be here asking questions. I need something from Gumley.'

'I'll go and get ready, then—I might even enjoy it.'

'Don't get carried away. You're going there for me and I don't crawl to people like Gumley. Watch your back. We've almost written off Gumley for your troubles, but you could just be walking into a trap—you think he'll lay off you because of David but a man as sick as he is can develop a twisted mind.'

And with those words ringing in his ears, John set off to visit his father-in-law, leaving Tollis to face Jamieson.

CHAPTER 9

There had been an unexpected rise in the temperature but some of the green areas that he drove past had patches of snow still where the sun had not yet reached. It was a pleasant drive along the coast road but John never really enjoyed it because at the end of it he had Gumley to face. Usually he had David with him and all he could think of was the duty that took him there.

Gumley had left his city home before John and Trish were married and now lived on the outskirts, near Cramond. In the last seven years Gumley had—surprisingly —never interfered with Gwen's upbringing of his grandson and had never gone near her home.

What sort of reception would he get? The old man was no fool and there was no plausible reason for this unscheduled call. The house overlooked the River Forth and had a clear view of the Fife coastline on the other side of the river.

It was set in sculptured grounds, with trees just inside the high walls, then lawns, but the house itself was set well back from any cultivation. Not even a border of flowers or a blade of grass came near the building itself, just a wide expanse of gravel that looked as if it was raked daily. Tollis had explained that Gumley was security conscious and the wide open spaces would ensure that any unwanted visitors would easily be spotted.

'He has cameras and spotlights fitted too. In fact, he has all that we recommend as far as security goes . . . not that he consulted Sentinel, of course.'

John looked for the cameras as he drove through the gates but he couldn't see them. Yet the front door stood open when he reached it and Garek, Gumley's 'nurse' and close friend, was at the top of the steps. The man had a long face and a bald head that looked too large for his slight frame. The only time John had seen him smile was when David was around and then Garek loosened up and had been known to crouch down to supervise the laying out of the model railway track that had been an expensive present from Gumley for David's birthday the year before.

'You didn't bring the boy,' Garek said after looking behind John into the empty car.

'Are you saying I can't come in without him?' He knew that Garek had no time for him or for anyone who upset his boss and on every visit John usually managed to anger Gumley in some way. Which meant he'd have to be tactful this time. Garek didn't answer but instead turned and led the way inside. Knowing what to expect, John had shed his heavy anorak before leaving the car but even so he felt the sweat break out on his body as the wave of heat hit him.

Gumley liked heat and every thermostat must have been at its highest setting, making every room uncomfortably hot. As he entered the large pleasant room where Gumley spent his days, it was like opening the door of an oven, and John saw that there was also a fire in there. Blazing logs were piled high in the huge grate and Gumley sat close to it with a woollen rug over his knees. John had not seen him since the end of summer and he was shocked at how the man's condition had deteriorated.

Gumley had once been short and stocky, but now the flesh had melted from his bones; his face had sunk, and his skin had wrinkled like used cling-film, but the expression in his eyes never changed. The small pale eyes, set under loose hooded eyelids, were as malevolent as ever, as if all the life force left to him was concentrated in one spot. He stretched out a hand and John was forced to accept this mock welcome. He felt the bones under the skin which was as brittle as dead leaves, and as if Gumley knew he was repelled by the contact, the old man smiled.

'Don't be deceived, Mr Leith. I'll be a long time in dying.'

The words were a whisper accompanied by a wheeze of breath and then John was motioned to the seat on the other side of the fire. 'I thought you'd bring the boy so that I could give him his birthday present,' Gumley added.

John edged the heavy leather chair back from the heat. 'We agreed after last year that you'd confine the gifts to Christmas. I won't have David getting expensive things.'

The last time he'd been adamant that the train set which needed an entire room to be laid in would stay with Gumley, and that David could play with it when he came to visit.

'Which was why I didn't send it,' Gumley said. 'I awaited your approval. Aren't you curious as to what I got him?'

John refused to be goaded and didn't answer.

'No? I have it here.' And Gumley drew a stiff sheaf of folded papers from under the rug on his knees, which made John wonder if the old man had had warning that he was coming, but that wasn't possible, surely?

'I've made my will and these are some of the investments that will go to the boy. As an accountant you might like to look them over.'

John made no attempt to take them. 'Give them to your lawyer,' he said stiffly.

He was at a disadvantage with sweat running down his face and he knew that Gumley was enjoying his discomfort.

'Bring Mr Leith a cold drink—or would you prefer something stronger?' Gumley asked as Garek hovered.

John stood up to take off his sweater. He pulled the chair further back from the fire and then sat down again, making Garek wait for an answer. 'I'll have tea,' he told Garek.

While they were alone John and Gumley faced each other with the usual tension between them. Gumley spoke first.

'You've had an injury or two, Mr Leith.' He never called John by his first name and he was smiling. John was certain that Gumley knew exactly what had been happening and that Tollis had been right about the old man keeping tabs on him. He didn't answer but waited to see what else Gumley would give away.

'The word is that you're in someone's bad books,' and he tutted like a taunting schoolmaster, only the effect was spoiled by the rattle in his chest.

'What do you know about it?' John asked, but Gumley spread his claw-like hands.

'I'm confined here. What could I know?' He was enjoying himself and he didn't hide the fact. He had never hidden his dislike of his son-in-law and John knew that if it wasn't for David, the man would never let him into the house.

'All right, play your games, but remember that if anything happens to me you'll never see David again. That's written in *my* will.' The anger at last had a target but he couldn't let it spill out. Forcing a calmness that he did not feel, he said, 'If you know what's going on, tell me.'

As if Gumley knew the effort it cost him, he smiled. 'You mean that Kramer and Tollis can't find that out for you? The Sentinel Agency with all its resources can't catch a few thugs?' He stopped and stared at John, eyes bright with malice.

'You know who they are, don't you?' John said.

Gumley let his body relax and he shrugged slightly. He had deliberately given away so much and he wasn't going to say any more.

Then Garek appeared with a tray and he glared at John as if sensing the atmosphere. He poured tea from a silver pot into a delicate china cup, the perfect manservant, who had once been Gumley's right-hand man in the underworld of crime. And John looked past him at the windows that filled an entire wall, at the polished dark wood of the furniture, the cream sofas and leaf-green carpet. There was a large bowl of rust-coloured chrysanthemums on a table and their pungent scent filled the room.

It looked like an illustration from a glossy magazine, designed by an expert and it was the sort of room that John would have been happy to live in. Gumley's tastes matched his own, right down to the pictures on the walls, and that gave him no comfort at all. He didn't want the tea either, but he took the cup from Garek and sipped from the egg-shell porcelain.

'We were discussing Mr Leith's accidents,' Gumley said, and a faint smile twitched at Garek's mouth.

'Garek and I have been very interested in the sequence of events and we have a small bet on the outcome.' Gumley had refused tea but he was sipping brandy from a balloon glass.

'You were right, of course. I may be stuck in this chair but I keep in touch.' Then his dark eyes flashed with anger. 'And I will continue to watch with interest what goes on because of the boy. You meddle in affairs that are dangerous and because of that the boy could be in danger as well.'

'You've got it all wrong. I'm not meddling in anything,' John said with equal anger, but Gumley was gasping for breath and Garek bent over him with an inhaler.

'You will not upset Mr Gumley,' Garek said over his shoulder.

'Don't give me that sick old man routine,' John snapped. 'If you really care about your grandson you'll help to put an end to all this. I don't know why I bothered to think you'd tell me anything.' And John stood up and made for the door.

It was the sound that Gumley made that made him pause and when he turned he saw that Gumley was laughing. It made his breathlessness worse and his skin darkened to purple, his eyes bulged and even Garek was alarmed, but Gumley just waved the man away.

'You've changed, John Leith. Adversity must suit you. You've been sitting on your backside for seven years but now a little prod has made you sit up. It is not nice to be a target, is it?' And his chest rattled as he laughed again. 'All right, I will do what I can but the territory has changed its boundaries. The rules that I knew no longer apply—do you know what I mean?'

Garek made sure that John understood. 'Mr Gumley has contacts but they are from the old days. And there is no honour among thieves, no matter what the books say.'

Gumley spoke again, although now he looked exhausted. 'Your uncle shouldn't waste his time sending men here. Tell him that from me.'

'Rees doesn't know I'm here,' John said evenly, but Gumley shook his head.

'I'm not talking about you. I mean the other one. Invading my privacy. Kramer had no right.'

Short sentences were gasped out in anger and John wondered if the old man would have a heart attack. Then Gumley reached out towards him, wanting him to come closer. John moved reluctantly and when he was within a couple of feet of him, Gumley moved surprisingly fast and clutched his wrist. His hand was cold, the flesh bloodless, and it was like being clutched by a corpse. Gumley seemed to guess what he was thinking and he smiled, with mucous stretching between his lips.

'Take the boy's present,' he whispered, indicating the bundle of papers on his lap. 'Honest investments, or as honest as I could make them. I'm dying slowly, John Leith. My heart can no longer send my blood through my arteries and my feet feel as if they are already dead. I can't walk and without a catheter I would sit in a puddle of my own urine . . . but I'm not dead yet, and don't you or your uncle forget it.'

He paused and sucked in another breath but his grip remained as firm as cold steel on John's wrist. 'And what you'll never be able to forget is that my blood is in your son. I will live on through the boy and every day of your life you'll see me in him. How do you like *that*, John Leith?' Then he released his hold and John took a step back, staring down at the old man. He had no answer so he spun on his heel and left the house wishing he'd never come.

He never wanted to return, but he would because the only way he could fight Gumley was to behave in a way that Gumley would never understand. He would honour the agreement he had made and continue to take David for the obligatory visits, but that didn't stop him wishing that Gumley was dead and in his grave.

After the heat of the house the cold bit into his sweat-drenched shirt and hurriedly he pulled on his sweater and anorak, threw the bundle of documents on the seat. Garek had followed him outside and he put his hand on the door before John could close it.

'When will you bring the boy? Mr Gumley has little time left now and it would make him happy to see the boy soon.'

'I'll phone you,' John said. He was disgusted that he'd found out so little from the visit and now he wanted to be gone.

'A trade,' Garek said quietly. 'Bring the boy soon and I'll do my best to help you.'

'Tell me now what happened to Toby and I'll consider it,' John said quickly. He gripped the steering-wheel tightly but tried not to let Garek see how important the answer would be to him. Garek hesitated and then shrugged. He seemed impervious to the icy wind that must be cutting into him.

'We don't really know. Of course, Mr Gumley knew he

was spying on us but it was a joke to pretend we were fooled. He enjoyed that very much but it would not have lasted much longer. Did you know that he came and asked for a job? Such a novice. Mr Gumley let him work in the grounds but one day he left and didn't come back. We had no reason to harm him, you know, so you can tell your uncle that he left here of his own free will.'

And as he drove off, John had the feeling that Garek was telling the truth; in fact he was dismally certain that Gumley had nothing to do with Toby's disappearance.

There was no need to rush back to town. Clare would already be in London, so he decided to keep going and pay Gwen a surprise visit. He would phone Tollis from there to let him know what he'd learned and that he wouldn't be back in town until the evening. As he drove, he kept remembering one thing that Gumley had said, that he had been content to sit on his backside for seven years.

It wasn't a comfortable feeling to know that Gumley of all people should have been able to read his character so well. It was like being naked, like coming out of a fog and seeing himself clearly for the first time and although it was possible to see that Gumley was right, hindsight didn't offer any explanation as to why he'd settled into such a rut. What had happened to his ambitions?

He turned into the road where Gwen had her bungalow hoping that she would be in, and the first thing he saw was the police car parked at her gate.

CHAPTER 10

'Someone broke in when we were out,' Gwen said. 'But they don't seem to have taken anything.' She looked dazed, as if she couldn't quite believe it and John had a sudden picture of his own flat flash through his mind and hoped that Gwen didn't have that destruction to face.

'Are you sure nothing's missing?' He looked down at her and for the first time in his life he felt protective towards his sister. She was seven years older and had always been the practical one, not the sort to be put out by anything, but now she looked small and vulnerable and her hands were shaking although they were clasped tightly together. He reached out and put his arm around her shoulders and Gwen leaned against him gratefully.

'Nothing as far as I can see,' she said. 'It's just that someone was in here, poking about, touching things. I'll have to scrub and polish . . .'

'Where's David?' he asked gently and she drew back and gave him a wobbly grin.

'Right beside the man dusting for fingerprints,' she said. 'He's not at all scared.' She seemed to give herself a shake and went to make tea. 'They broke a pane in the back door —that's the only damage as far as I can see. You just don't expect to come back from the shops to find strangers have been in your house, John.' She dropped the kettle and leaned on the sink. 'Oh God, I forgot, you know exactly how it feels.'

He nodded. Later she would wonder what might have happened if the men had stayed in the house, still been there when she opened the door.

'I'll go and see if there's anything they can tell me,' he

told her. 'You sit there and drink your tea and I'll be back in a minute.'

He went upstairs, following the sound of voices, and found two men in the spare bedroom and David lying on the bed watching every move they made.

'Go and keep Gwen company while I speak to the policemen,' he told his son and waited until the boy had left before turning to the two men. He introduced himself but they were not very forthcoming.

'Your sister says nothing's been taken,' one said, shrugging. 'And from the look of things we think they didn't have time to look around. This is the only room that has been tossed about.'

It was the room he used when he stayed there. He had a mental image of the men going through the house, ignoring the bedroom that was Gwen's and the others that were obviously boys' rooms. So that left this one as the one they needed to seach. And they'd been very thorough. He looked at the drawers that had been pulled out, the bedding heaped on the floor, the slashed mattress, and felt cold. They must be desperate to do this in daylight and desperate men are violent—he already knew that these were. If Gwen and David had been here . . .

'Have there been other break-ins reported around here? This is such a quiet area, off the main road . . .'

One of the men made a face as he considered that. 'You'd be surprised at the sort of places that get done over, but yes, this street isn't a likely place, mainly because it's a dead end and there's not much cover. They were probably cruising around and took a chance.'

They began to pack up their equipment and Gwen called up to ask if they wanted tea. 'Never say no,' one said.

John wished Gwen had just let them leave. He didn't want her telling them that his flat had been broken into as well, or that his car had been tampered with on his last visit, but to his relief Gwen didn't mention either, probably because it didn't occur to her that the incidents could be connected, as he was certain they were. Gumley had accused him of meddling and thereby endangering David and it looked as if he was right.

As soon as the plain-clothes men had departed John put the room to rights and hauled the damaged mattress out to the garage. He phoned a glazier to come and replace the broken pane in the door and at the same time called Tollis to tell him what had happened.

'I don't want to leave them tonight. It's just beginning to sink in and Gwen's pretty shaken.'

'Why not bring them up to town, to a hotel for a day or two, or to Elmwood?' Tollis suggested.

And to John's surprise Gwen didn't put up much of an argument.

'Stay with Rees for a day or so,' he urged. 'There's nothing to keep you here.'

She hesitated. 'I hate to think I'm letting those . . . people . . . drive me out of my own home.'

'Look, we can let the police know that you're going to be away and they'll keep an eye on the house.'

It was the wrong thing to say. 'You don't think they'll come back?' she said, alarmed.

'Of course not—the detectives said they were just chancers, but you'd feel better if someone was checking the house, wouldn't you?'

Still she hesitated. She fussed around, straightening cushions, looking around her as if seeking some contamination left by the intruders. Then she shivered. 'I don't think I'll ever feel that this is my home again and I'll be glad to sell it. Let's make a fresh pot of tea . . . I can't make decisions right now.'

David was full of questions and seemed to be looking forward to telling his friends about the incident, so obviously he wasn't at all upset about it. John sent him off to watch TV so that he and Gwen could talk.

They sat at the kitchen table, Gwen holding her mug of tea with both hands as if she needed the warmth from it. 'It could have been worse, couldn't it?' she said suddenly and John realized that her brain was functioning again and she was working things out.

'Maybe not,' he said. 'I've heard that most burglars will run rather than face the families coming back unexpectedly. They just want to make a quick raid and then leave.'

Gwen regarded him with disbelief in her eyes. 'But your flat was broken into . . . and there were those men at your car . . .' Then her eyes went to the bruising on his face and he saw the horror in her eyes. 'Your accident?' She spilled her tea and the hot liquid ran over the table and dribbled on the floor. 'Don't tell me that was part of all of this?'

What could he say? 'I don't understand it any more than you do,' he said quietly, 'but maybe it would be a good idea if you and David were to come back with me like Tollis suggested. I've already decided that David will be living with me,' he went on. 'And if it makes it any easier for you we'll all go to Elmwood now. Just pack his bags—it's as easy as that.'

She made up her mind and nodded, but her eyes had a haunted look that made John clench his jaw with anger. The bastards. They were inflicting so much grief, and now his sister would probably not be able to sleep at nights.

'And it might be a good idea to phone Greg and put him in the picture. I think he'll want you in Aberdeen right away.'

She was calm now and shook her head vigorously. 'No, the boys will be coming home for Christmas and I won't be frightened off by a bunch of crooks, but I will stay at Elmwood for a few days.' And she reached out and put her hand on his arm. 'I'm glad David's going to be with you. And it won't be nearly as bad as you think.'

'Right,' John said briskly. 'Now we have to tell him— how do you think he'll take it?'

'He'll be no problem. Of course you don't have to tell him it's permanent . . . not yet. It can be a trip to his Uncle Rees and he always loves that. In fact, that might be the best way—just enough clothes and things for a holiday and you can pick up the rest later.'

And just two hours later John was driving off with Gwen and his son, leaving the house securely locked up. John glanced at David who was dressed in fresh clothes, his hair still damp after the bath that Gwen had insisted he take. His son was his responsibility now—sooner than he'd planned. He wasn't sure how he felt about it yet except that deep down he knew it was something that he should have done a long, long time ago.

CHAPTER 11

It took an hour to reach Elmwood where Rees and his housekeeper Janet were expecting them. John had phoned from Gwen's to explain what had happened and warned Rees that as yet David thought he was staying for a week or so.

'You can all stay as long as you like. Goodness knows, we've plenty of room.'

And as soon they got inside the door Janet whisked David and Gwen off to the kitchen. 'Boys are always hungry,' she said in her soft Highland accent, 'and Gwen and I can have a nice chat.' John followed Rees into his study.

'Tollis has been on the phone—he should have told me he was sending you to Gumley's. Anyway, I said you'd probably call him again later. You will be staying tonight?'

'Probably.'

Rees's earlier enthusiasm had died away, as if he couldn't sustain any great emotion for long and now his shoulders were stooped as he went to pour out two whiskies for them. His skin looked unhealthily muddy, grey-tinged, and there was a tremor in his fingers as he held the heavy crystal decanter.

John didn't comment, but wondered if it had been a good idea to impose a young boy on him at short notice. As if reading his thoughts, Rees smiled slightly as he handed over the glass.

'It's time there was a child in the house again. Janet will spoil him, of course, and so will I, but I feel like his grandfather, and grandparents are allowed that privilege. Gwen can have a break, get into town if she feels like it.'

He sipped from his glass, swirled the liquid around as he studied it and then took a deeper gulp. He was out of business clothes, dressed instead in a favourite old cardigan that was thin at the elbows. 'How was Gumley, then? I swear if I ever get in that state I won't cling to life.'

'Malice keeps Gumley alive. When he stops hating the world he'll be gone. David is the only human being he has any real feeling for and I think it's genuine . . . even if it's only because he knows that David will keep his genes going.'

'I expect you're right,' Rees said wearily. 'A man needs to feel that there has been something worthwhile in his life. Did he say anything about Toby?' As Rees asked the question John got the feeling that it was what Rees had been wanting to ask since he came in the door.

He leaned forward, elbows on knees. He felt incredibly tired but accepted that his body had taken a lot of knocks and shocks in the last few days and that it was natural for it to protest.

'He knew all along that Toby was a plant but denies knowing anything about his disappearance. He said Toby went and that's the last they saw of him, but he's promised to try to get some information from contacts he has. I think he will do that.' He drained the last of the Scotch and then stood up and stretched.

'I'm going to have an early night, Rees, right after supper, and I think you should too.'

Rees looked up at him and then spoke quietly. 'Janet and the doctor have both been nagging so there's no need for you to start. But you're right. We all need an early night . . . we never know what tomorrow will bring.'

John phoned Tollis later, repeating what he'd told Rees and explaining what had happened at Gwen's. 'So they're still looking for something. I wish to hell I knew what it is that they want from me.'

'We'll find out,' Tollis assured him. 'I have a feeling that we're reaching a crisis point. They are desperately searching for something and it just may bring them out into the open. It might be a good idea for you to stay where you are.'

'Well, don't hold your breath about that—I'm coming up to town tomorrow and I want to be in on any developments. Gwen will look after David and he'll keep Rees busy, but I can't help wondering if Elmwood is secure. Do you think these people are likely to come here?'

'Rees has every security device you can think of but I'll send someone down as a back-up. Come up here in the morning and I'll try to find something for you to do.'

David was asleep when John looked in on him and he stood for a few moments looking down on his son, wondering what he'd let himself in for.

The boy was used to having Gwen as mother-substitute and she knew all the little things about David that it would take him a long time to find out. In the meantime they had this interlude in Rees's home but he'd have to arrange for David's schooling and many other things. It would mean adjustments for both of them; David would have to make new friends, learn to cope with a father who knew nothing about being a father. He reached out and touched his son's dark hair. The first priority was to make sure that David was safe. He spent half the night tossing restlessly as he dreamed about the faceless men who were mucking up his life.

It was during breakfast the next morning that Janet burst in with the news that 'that man from Gumley was at the door'. It was Garek, in his usual sombre black suit and with raindrops glistening on his bald head.

'For the boy,' he said, laying a basket just inside the

hallway. 'Mr Gumley promised the boy a puppy for Christmas but after what happened yesterday . . .'

'How the hell did you find out about that? And how did you know David was here?'

But Garek didn't answer; he was smiling down at David who was already investigating the basket, exclaiming about the golden Labrador pup which was wriggling to lick his face.

'Can I keep him?' he said looking from John to Rees, who shrugged. The pup got loose and lolloped off with David chasing and when John turned back to Garek he was astonished to see him grinning. It changed the man completely.

'Would you like some coffee, Mr Garek?' Rees said politely, as if Garek was an ordinary visitor.

And still with the remnants of the smile on his face, Garek nodded.

'It is a bitch, tell the boy,' he said. 'Labradors are gentle and this one has a good pedigree.'

They returned to the breakfast table and watched Rees fetch a fresh cup and saucer, pour coffee for Garek.

'Well, how did you know about the break-in at my sister's home?' John persisted.

Garek took his time in replying. 'Mr Gumley was concerned for the boy, so he sent men to watch over the house.' He picked up his coffee cup and looked as if he would say no more than that.

'Then you know who broke in?'

'We think so. Two who hire out for money. They are not clever men.'

'And?' It was obvious that Rees was losing his temper but Garek seemed not to notice because he simply shrugged as if the men were of no importance. 'Brothers, surname Grey. They will work for anyone who pays,' and Garek made a grimace as if he found that to mention their name was distasteful to him. 'It won't get you anywhere to know this. No one will be traced by questioning them.'

Rees sat back down, nodding. 'You're probably right.'

Garek put down his cup. 'I know I am because they admitted it was arranged through a contact—they are too stupid to lie and they have no loyalty.' He stood up. 'Now I must go.' He looked at John. 'Mr Gumley would like to see the boy, soon.'

And he didn't wait for an answer. It was as if an order from Gumley would be obeyed without question.

'Just a minute,' John said. 'If you were keeping watch on Gwen's house, why didn't you stop them getting in?'

'Because the boy was not there and therefore not in danger. We wanted to see what they were looking for—you would have done the same.'

'And what were they looking for?'

Garek smiled slightly. 'They didn't find it.'

'You spoke to them?'

'They were afraid to say anything—that tells you a lot.'

It told John that two hired villains were scared of who was paying them; more scared than they were of Garek.

'Violent masters, I think,' Garek murmured solemnly. 'Things are very different these days.'

John let Rees see the man out and got ready to drive to Edinburgh.

'I'm going to town,' he told Rees after Garek had driven away. 'What do you suppose Garek has done with those two men?'

Rees shrugged. 'Turned them loose with a warning and a kick up the backside, I suppose. He's hardly likely to turn them over to the police. So be careful.'

'I'm tired of being told to be careful, Rees. I'd rather be told how to find out who hired those men.'

Rees sighed and turned away. Rain battered against the window in a sudden squall. 'I'll call Tollis and tell him about the Greys—he'll know what to do,' he said, closing the subject.

It was as if he'd switched off and John wondered if Garek had really let them go with no more than a warning.

'Rees, Tollis asked if I'd be keeping an eye on the business while you take a break. Is that all right with you?'

'It's what I hoped,' Rees said with a tired smile. He moved closer to the window to stare at the rain slanting across the lawn and didn't turn as John left the room. David hardly noticed that his father was leaving. He and Gwen were arranging bedding in the basket for the pup who had already disgraced herself by leaving puddles in Janet's spotless kitchen.

'What are you going to call her?' John asked.

'He can't make up his mind,' Gwen said. 'Will you be home for supper?'

'I don't know. I may stay in town but I'll phone you later.' He wondered if he should mention that someone would be coming to keep an eye on Elmwood, but decided that there was no point in upsetting her. Gwen was not stupid and it wouldn't take her long to work out that every other place he'd been had been searched and that, apart from the Kramer building itself, Elmwood was the next obvious choice.

As soon as he reached the office block he went to Rees's office and set about the stack of post and messages that were waiting for him. Most of it could be handled by Rees's secretary but one name on the list of phone messages caught his eye. Arran Sinclair had called and would ring back. Where had he heard that name recently?

He reached into a drawer and pulled out the copies of the files he'd taken to Gwen's and then flipped through them. Rees and Tollis had mentioned the name Carrick in connection with the Sinclair estate and Hugh Carrick was one of those names on the files. He read the details and then closed the pages. The man was selling a piece of land for development but there were some details still to be settled and the sale had not yet been put into action. Probably the call was about that and now he'd have to deal with it.

He worked steadily on, intending to join Tollis for a coffee break to find out what Jamieson had said the day before. Then Rees's secretary put her head around the door.

'Miss Sinclair again—do you want me to take it?'

He was almost finished and he'd have to talk to her sometime. 'No, put her through.'

There was a pause and then a cool voice said, 'This is Arran Sinclair, Mr Leith. I'm leaving shortly to drive to Edinburgh and I had intended calling in to see Mr Kramer about what progress is being made on the sale. My stepfather isn't here very often so I haven't heard anything.'

She had a nice voice with hardly any accent but it didn't sound at all friendly.

'I'm looking after things for a few days and I'd be happy to see you, Miss Sinclair. Would you like to come to the office, or perhaps you'd allow me to take you to lunch?'

They arranged to meet at the George Hotel at one p.m. and as soon as she hung up, John phoned the hotel and booked a table. That gave him a couple of hours, so he had plenty of time to see Tollis—and change into one of his new suits. The George was no place for jeans, nor were Rees's clients.

'Lunch with Arran Sinclair,' Tollis said.

'You know her?'

'Of her. Rees used to go there when her father was alive,

shooting and fishing weekends. He often talks about the estate and I think he was sad that bits of it were getting sold off. The stepfather seems a bit of a lad.'

'That'll be Hugh Carrick.'

'He married the widow Sinclair very soon after her husband died, according to Rees, and then promptly moved out. The daughter runs the place and I think there's a son, but he couldn't get on with Carrick so he went off too. Carrick has a reputation for gambling—hence the need for cash, no doubt. That's quite a job for a young woman.'

'And I wonder how she feels about the land sale when she and her brother must have expected to inherit it?'

Tollis grinned. 'You're about to find out.'

'Mm. What did Jamieson have to say?'

'Not much—and Rees phoned about the two men that Garek named. He'll bring them in for questioning.'

John got to his feet. 'Right, that gives me time to call in at my office before I meet Arran Sinclair. I'll pick up my post and later on I'll arrange for someone to shift the files up to Rees's place. Somehow I have the feeling that I'll be there for some time.'

'Rees will be difficult to live with, I think—he has no interest in anything but the business,' Tollis muttered. 'He practically lived in this building.'

'Like you do?'

Tollis smiled grimly. 'Then take warning. It gets to you.'

'I don't know if I'm the type,' John said lightly, but in a way it was a gentle hint that he was not yet making any commitment to take over from his uncle. Moving his stuff into the building was an emergency measure, a convenience, but as yet he couldn't see himself as managing such a large concern. And there was another reason that he didn't want to admit even to himself. He was caught up in the intrigue to such an extent that he'd not thought of his own clients for days. As Tollis said, it got to you. And he was almost used to going from car to the safety of buildings, walking in the open as little as possible. He still had the feeling that eyes were watching his every move and now it had become a habit to look in his mirror to see what cars were behind him.

However, soon the Grey brothers would no longer be a threat and unless there were more to take their place . . . It was not a nice way to live, but unless he wanted to go into hiding, he had no choice.

Arran Sinclair was not at all as he'd imagined. Somehow he had thought of her as capable of manual work, horsey and bossy, but the girl who turned up punctually at the George had curly fair hair that was cut short and long legs that were in knee-high black boots under a black mini skirt. She wore a high-necked white polo jumper under a black leather blouson jacket and her skin was glowing with health. She moved like an athlete, a young woman in complete control of herself, knowing that all the men in the room were turning their heads to watch her go by, and thoroughly enjoying it.

They had a corner table in the ornate dining-room and no sooner had they taken their seats than a waiter was there with the menus, so John still hadn't said more than 'Pleased you could come.' But from the first moment when she shook his hand, he'd been aware that Miss Arran Sinclair was not going to be an easy lunch companion because for some reason she was hostile.

After they'd ordered she made it clear she wanted to get down to business. 'Now, what's happening to our land sale?'

There it was again, that antagonism in her look, so John was blunt.

'Absolutely nothing. Mr Carrick hasn't given the final

go-ahead. In fact, he's cancelled several appointments and my uncle is beginning to think he's having second thoughts.'

'Huh. He won't be doing that.'

She stabbed at the white tablecloth with the point of her steak knife and then doodled with it, drawing precise squares. Her blue eyes seemed even bluer with anger as she dropped it and leaned her elbows on the table.

'He's holding out for more, I expect—more land, I mean. Is that on your advice?'

John was taken aback. 'My advice? I've never met him.'

'Your uncle's, then.'

'Rees told me that Mr Carrick has not been in the office —their conversations were by phone.'

She blinked and seemed puzzled. 'You don't know my stepfather.' It was a flat statement rather than a question. John shook his head.

'I don't understand. I thought he was getting one of his cronies to handle the sale.'

John took pity on her and spoke quietly. 'He phoned Kramer Property and we arranged the survey—or rather, my uncle did. I'm not even part of the firm but my uncle isn't well and I've sort of stepped in to run things.'

To give her her due, Arran gave a small grin of apology and then shrugged. 'Let's start from scratch, then. I came here ready to put you firmly in your place because Hugh is trying to screw every penny out of the estate and I wasn't about to let that happen.'

'Can you stop him?'

'Oh yes,' she said calmly. 'Hugh only had control until my brother Lewis and I came of age. The estate was held in trust for us. We own it, Mr Leith.'

'Ahh, I see daylight—I think. Then why sell at all? I take it you don't really want to?'

The waiter arrived with their steaks and Arran talked as she ate, mouth full and with obvious enjoyment. 'Of course I don't, but it will mean that Hugh will stay away from now on. It's blackmail, you see—he gets the proceeds of the land sale and that's the last he'll ever get.'

John remembered what Tollis had said about Carrick's gambling habit and wondered if the man could be trusted to settle for a one-off bribe. And as if Arran read his mind she agreed.

'I can't trust him but we're getting it all drawn up legally. So you can see why I'm keen to get it over with.'

'Well, as far as I can see the only detail we need is a decision on the stretch of land that runs along the river. That would add a great deal to the price.'

'And Hugh knows that's out of the question. Can't you see, that's why he's stalling? A great part of our income is from paying guests and we must protect our fishing rights. The land that Hugh's getting is on the other side, blocked off from us by high ground, so if he insists on developing it, it won't spoil the view but I'd still keep it if I could.'

'I'd love to see it,' John said, meaning it. 'My uncle has been there but I don't suppose you remember him.'

She thought about that. 'I don't remember the name.'

'He was a friend of your father and I can assure you Rees would never help Carrick to cheat you.'

'You must come, then, and please call me Arran.' She had a wide smile and all the antagonism was gone. 'I wonder why Hugh chose your firm? He surely couldn't know your uncle would know our place.'

'I expect it was because of our reputation and he wanted the best deal he could get. It will raise a very great deal of money, you know.'

She frowned. 'Money that we could make good use

of, believe me. But it's going to be worth it to get rid of him.'

John felt he could put a delicate question without offending her. 'What about your mother, Arran? Is this what she wants too?'

It was none of his business but he knew that Rees would have tried to offer this girl advice too.

She hesitated before answering and her candid blue eyes seemed to assess him. Then, as if deciding she could trust him, she raised expressive eyebrows and was completely frank about the situation between her mother and Hugh Carrick.

'My mother is scared of him. He married her when she was vulnerable, after my father died, but he rarely came to the estate once he managed to get an income from it. Now he only appears when he's short of funds. I agreed to buy him off mainly for my mother's sake.'

John liked her. She was a strong girl with bags of character but he sensed that her mother wasn't the only one who was scared of Hugh Carrick. 'And your brother? Won't he come back now?'

She shrugged eloquently. 'He's doing well, but he might if Hugh was out of the picture.'

They were at the coffee stage of the meal and the dining-room was emptying. John stretched his legs under the table and leaned back in the plush chair. 'When are you going back?' he asked.

'Tomorrow morning.' Arran raised her delicately arched eyebrows. 'Why don't you drive back with me and come to lunch?'

'Is there any chance that your stepfather will be there? Then we could get things moving.'

She shook her head. 'Lord, I hope not. Lately he's been bringing some weird people with him. They sit up half the night playing cards and I think one of them is interested in

the land. Hugh's shown him around but he didn't enjoy it.'
She giggled like a teenager although she had to be around
twenty-five. 'He wore a suit and borrowed wellingtons and
had to walk miles through the snow.'

'He'll have competition. That land will draw offers—did
he look the wealthy type?'

She shrugged. 'I hardly spoke to him. He was quiet but
you couldn't help noticing him at the same time.'

John got the impression that she hadn't liked the man
and she confirmed it.

'I'll be glad when it's all settled and then I won't have
people like that in the house.'

'Pity your stepfather won't be there—I'd like to meet
him.'

'It wouldn't be any fun, I can assure you. Hugh can be
charming but only in his own interests.'

'But it would be—in his interest, I mean. After all,
he's relying on Kramer's to get him half a million, with
luck.'

'As much as that?' She looked dismayed.

'It could be much more. You don't have to give in to
him, you know,' John said, leaning forward. 'There must
be a way that your lawyers can keep him away from your
mother.'

She compressed her lips and shook her head again. 'My
mother won't put up a fight. She rarely leaves her rooms
these days. The doctor says she's going downhill slowly and
the best thing we can do is to see she isn't upset in any
way. So you see, I have no choice.' She spoke flatly; a realist
who had made her decision and would stick to it no matter
how it hurt her financially.

'Then I'll do my best to see that it's painless, and I *would*
like to come to lunch tomorrow.'

And as he said to Tollis later, 'Carrick, according to
Arran Sinclair, has some "weird" friends. He's a gambler

and seems pretty ruthless about how he gets his money. Isn't there a remote chance that—'

Tollis interrupted. 'You had his file with you when you went to Gwen's and you're wondering if that's what they're looking for? Why? He has his own copy.' Tollis made a steeple with his fingers and tapped the sides of his nose. 'Still, there's no harm in reacting to hunches—I do it all the time. You go up there and have your lunch and I'll do some digging of my own. Let's have a look at Hugh Carrick's background—and his friends. If nothing else, it will stop me from going crazy.'

CHAPTER 12

He spent some time going through Rees's files to see if there was any other reference to the Sinclair estate and then got a call from Tollis.

'Jamieson's here and he'd like to talk to you,' he said drily.

'I'll be right down.'

Tollis was behind his desk, looking bad-tempered, and the policeman was sitting in a hard-backed chair to one side, looking inscrutable.

'Mr Leith,' the Inspector said as if he'd been waiting patiently, 'I thought it would be more convenient to have a chat here rather than ask you to come to the police station.' He shifted round in the chair as John pulled another forward. The policeman was in a well-cut dark blue suit; he looked relaxed, but his eyes were alert. 'We haven't picked up those two men yet but we should find them soon. Maybe you could look at some photographs and see if you can pick them out.'

He spread a dozen photos on the desk and John moved closer. He saw one of the men straight away. 'Him,' he said. He studied the rest but he had never really seen the second man for any length of time. 'Not the other one, I'm afraid.'

'That's fine.' Jamieson gathered the prints up without telling him if he'd picked out a Grey. 'There's not much other progress to report—my colleagues in the Lanark force tell me that you sister has had some trouble too. Quite an epidemic, isn't it?'

'Did they leave fingerprints. Can you arrest them?'

'No prints. They're not very bright but they do know to

wear gloves. I really wanted to talk to your uncle but it can wait.' Jamieson said that in a preoccupied tone of voice and then he brightened. 'But Tollis has explained that you don't work for this firm, so that opens a whole new angle, doesn't it? *You* are the target and not this company. That's not a comfortable situation to be in but it will sort itself out.'

John said nothing and he had the feeling that the policeman didn't expect him to reply.

Jamieson had turned back to Tollis and he spoke more briskly. 'But a missing man won't. The trouble is that we don't know where to start looking—that's your problem too, I take it?'

Tollis gave a very brief nod but said nothing and Jamieson got to his feet. He didn't have Tollis's bulk or height and he moved like a cat, turning on the balls of his feet to face John. 'So it's patience on both counts and I'm really looking forward to the next episode in yours. You do realize that there will be one?' His eyes sparkled with genuine amusement, but John didn't find it funny.

Jamieson walked to the door, buttoning his overcoat, tucking his scarf neatly inside it. 'Watch your back, Mr Leith, and we'll do our utmost to find the elusive Grey brothers,' he said as he left.

Tollis was out of his chair quicker than John had seen him move before. The big man stopped at the door and glared at it as if to send some message to Jamieson's back. 'Blast the man, he's enjoying this and even when I don't tell him anything I still get the feeling that he's read my thoughts anyway.'

'You didn't tell him that Toby was at Gumley's,' John said.

'No. And I damn well should have but that would have meant explaining that it was Rees's doing.'

'Couldn't Toby's disappearance have started something off? For Christ's sake, Tollis, you're supposed to know about these things and you're ignoring Gumley's background and the fact that he hates my guts.'

'No, I'm not. I haven't been sitting idly here, you know, and I understand how you feel. Take it from me that Gumley is out of the game and has been for years. Now, I could do with a drink and I want to get out of here for a bit. Are you coming?'

They only went to the corner of the street, but as they walked Tollis took great gulps of air. 'I've been stuck in there for days. I can't stand bloody inaction—I never wanted a desk job and at times like this I envy the men who can get outside and do something positive.'

His hands were thrust deep in the pockets of his old raincoat so that the front drooped to his knees, and he needed a shave.

Once inside the pub, he sucked down most of the first pint in a couple of swallows. John let him talk, realizing that Tollis, the man of few words, needed just this once to let the words pour out.

'Rees never complained, you know, when he ran Sentinel, but sometimes I wonder how he ever managed it. You send men out on jobs—even ordinary ones—and you wonder if something unexpected will turn up. I actually used to like the excitement of the job, but not any more.' He paused and set down the empty glass. 'I've got the men on nothing else but looking for Toby, but so far nobody knows anything. That's unusual, you know. There hasn't been so much as a whisper and that's raising Mike's hopes . . .' He stared morosely inot the glass but didn't go for another one and John tried to change the subject.

'Is there anything new on Hugh Carrick? If I'm going to the estate for lunch tomorrow I'd like to know what to look for.'

Tollis didn't seem all that interested in the Carrick angle, but he pulled out a notebook. 'He's based in London these days, although he likes to visit the clubs in Glasgow from time to time. His friends are the sort who share his gambling tastes. He's a sort of middle-aged playboy; smart clothes, flashes money around to impress people, owns a sea-going yacht. He'll come to a sticky end if his money ever runs out but I can't see how he can have anything to do with you. Carrick rarely comes to Edinburgh, as far as I know.'

'But—if we're clutching at straws—Carrick has a yacht so he could slip into Granton and it's not a long drive to the estate from there. You did say he liked impressing his friends and what better way to bring them?'

'Then what? If we put down on paper a list of the information we have—and I've tried that—all we get is a lot of "ifs" and "maybes". Perhaps Carrick, pushed for ready cash, got desperate for a quick sale on his land and so he sends heavies to break into your office, gets you run off the road, wrecks your flat, Gwen's place? Nothing was taken. The only connection is that survey report you had, and Carrick already had a copy of that. Clutching at straws is right. To be honest, I'm more concerned about Toby than what's happening to you at this moment.'

They stared at each other, Tollis grim-faced.

Then John stood up. 'I'd better get back to the office and see how the property business is doing. I may stay in the flat tonight.' And there would be no Clare there to keep him company.

'And Rees has plenty of security at Elmwood, so you don't have to worry about them being there,' Tollis said shortly. 'Come down tonight if you feel you need some company. I'll have to stay by the phone. Something's got to happen soon.'

John made his phone calls first; Gwen was happy enough to be left in charge of David and she said Rees was very quiet.

'He hasn't mentioned going back to work.' She sounded

a bit concerned about him. 'Has he got something on his mind, John? I've never seen him so . . . introspective. Rees was always so sure of himself.'

'He's tired,' John said. And blaming himself for Toby's disappearance, but Gwen knew nothing of that.

The rest of the day was taken up with phone calls to agents explaining about his new address and he made a note to send out a circular to others. He conferred with Rees's secretary about any appointments that could be cancelled and then sorted out his own files in an empty room along the corridor from Rees's office. There was no time to think about the visit next day to the Sinclair estate.

At seven he slipped out and collected a carry-out from an Italian place and took it with him to share with Tollis. They ate it with plastic cutlery, dumped the remains in a waste bin that was already overflowing.

'Don't you ever go home?' John asked.

Tollis shrugged. 'It's only a place to sleep and I can do that here. I need somewhere—have to know that it's there —but sometimes I wonder why I bother to pay the mortgage.' He yawned and stretched his arms high above his head. 'It's only a flat in the student area. Where will you start looking for your house?'

They discussed housing costs and the best areas, schools for David, but both were aware that they were avoiding the topics uppermost in their minds. At ten, John said he was off to bed and Tollis went back behind his desk, his eyes rarely away from the phone that so far had not rung. And John thought that waiting for something to happen was far worse than having it happen.

He tried to put himself into the opposition's place, into the mind of the man who was so desperate to recover something he mistakenly thought John had. Surely his patience was running out and now that the Grey brothers were no longer able to walk the streets, he had no back-up. Would he come out into the open, or decide that whatever he was searching for was in fact lost?

Wait and see was the only answer. But why should he wait? He reached for the phone and rang Gumley's number and it rang for some time before Garek answered.

'Mr Leith?'

'Those two men—do you have any clues where they are?'

'That depends on how scared they are. If they had any sense they will be long gone, but they were not very clever.'

'Scared of what?'

'Scared of whoever employed them, because they failed —who knows? They made that very clear—that the man who paid them would bury them under the new by-pass or one of the new hotels—he wasn't very specific but the threat was enough. Yet to employ such fools means that the man who did so does not know much about who is for hire in Edinburgh or he would have chosen better—yes? It follows that the man you would very much like to meet is not local. More than likely he met them in a pub and offered payment and they didn't realize what they were getting into. Surely Tollis has worked that out?'

Tollis was thinking no further than Toby Cairns.

John was about to hang up when he decided to ask one more question.

'Does the name Carrick mean anything to you?'

Garek didn't answer immediately and John was about to repeat the question when he thought he heard the man laughing.

'Carrick.' Garek spoke soberly enough now. 'Yes, I have heard of Mr Carrick. He likes to gamble but never quite manages to make a profit. I hope you don't count him as a friend, Mr Leith.'

John heard the phone being put down and then the dialling tone sounded. Damn the man. He never answered a question directly and John almost wished he hadn't phoned. He needed a good night's sleep, but now sleep was the last thing that was possible.

He went into the sitting-room and took a bundle of blank writing paper from Rees's bureau, and then he took Tollis's suggestion and began to write down all that had happened so far.

None of it was any different from what he'd told Tollis and nothing at all pointed to Hugh Carrick being implicated. So he would go to the Sinclair estate with an open mind and find out all he could about the man. At least that was positive, even if it only ruled Carrick out.

He screwed up all the notes and dropped them in the waste basket. Tollis wasn't the only one to have gut feelings. Although he'd never met Hugh Carrick, the very mention of the man's name made his nerves tingle.

CHAPTER 13

He had arranged to meet Arran Sinclair at her hotel for breakfast and then they'd drive separately to the estate.

'It will give you time to look around before lunch,' she said before they set off, and in fact they made good time and arrived before eleven.

The main house was red sandstone but extensions and other outbuildings gave it the appearance of a sprawling mass that had followed no architect's plan. It was set among mature trees that came close to the house but there were no gardens as such, except for some shrubs and lawns that might be a concession to paying guests.

He followed Arran's car around the tarred narrow road to the back where there was a large parking area. This was the working side of the house with farm vehicles, tarpaulin-covered pony carts, a truck and a couple of five-year-old cars nosing up against workshops.

Stables stood on the other side of the open square and two horses poked their heads over the half-doors when they heard them drive in. He saw several cats and a couple of dogs moving about and the ringing sound of a man hammering on metal.

In general the place looked a bit run down, with a weed here and there growing up through cracked paving and the paintwork on the buildings was chipped, but there was a comfortable feeling about it too, that this was a busy working estate. He could hear men's voices in some of the sheds and as he climbed out of his car he heard the scrape of metal-tacked boots approaching. The man nodded at Arran and looked with suspicion at John. Arran introduced him.

'This is Mr John Leith. John, this is my manager, James

McNeil.' John reached out and shook the hand of a small man with cords tucked into serviceable leather boots, who had paused with hands on hips. It was bitterly cold, with an icy wind sweeping across the flat land below the hills, but the neck of his checked shirt, under an old tweed jacket, was open. He seemed impervious to the cold although his cheeks and nose shone red and his breath condensed as it froze.

'Aye,' was all he said as he gripped John's hand firmly.

He was of that age that could be anything between late fifties to seventies.

'We get all sorts pulling in here when they get lost—you can't be too careful, and when I heard the cars . . .' He bustled past John with the gait of a man who never takes time to rest and led the way into the back porch which was full of boots, rubber and leather, and oilskins hanging from hooks on one wall. He cleaned his feet on a metal scraper and then went along a corridor floored with very old linoleum. Arran smiled at John.

'He probably has reports for me. Let's see what he wants first.' And as he followed Arran along the corridor, he heard the murmur of voices from the various rooms that they passed.

'Office girls and house staff,' Arran explained. 'We're pretty quiet just now but we take on more people in the late spring when the guests come . . . We get some in the winter too, but nearer Christmas.'

McNeil paused to listen and put in his bit. 'I manage the outside and Miss Arran does the inside . . . but she likes to look over my shoulder too, whiles.'

He threw a grin back at John, showing dentures that gleamed white against weathered skin, but that was not all he revealed. When he spoke of Arran it was with fondness, love even, as if she was a daughter in everything but name. His old employer's child and therefore worthy of loyalty and a lot more besides. And if she interfered in what he considered his job as manager of the estate, he would tolerate it. It was all in that smile and John felt he was already getting the sense of the place. They stopped at a darkly varnished door which McNeil opened without knocking. He poked his head inside and then went all the way in.

'I just wanted the stock book,' he said, deftly finding what he wanted from the clutter on a desk. Then he eased by them and strode off back the way they'd come. Arran giggled suddenly and apologized for the state of the room.

'I keep hoping to get all this on to a computer but something else always eats up the cash first, and so far I haven't managed to buy one. Would you like coffee?'

'If it's no trouble, yes.'

'I'll take you along to the kitchen then, and I'll go and change into my working gear. And if we're lucky there might be hot scones. And I want to show you round so we'll need to find you some boots.'

He had anticipated her to the extent that he'd put on a heavy jersey and anorak and after they'd drunk freshly made coffee in the huge kitchen and Arran had changed into denims and a fluffy blue jumper, she handed him a pair of wellingtons that were identical to those lent him by Betty not so long ago.

He perched on a wooden chair to tuck his trousers inside them while Arran checked over the lunch menu.

'McNeil eats with us—that's to give us a chance to talk business but it's informal—we eat in here.'

She pointed to the long scrubbed table where a plump woman was trimming pastry from the edge of a pie. 'Jenny is our cook and does lots more besides. When we've no visitors we eat plain fare at this time, but it's our main meal of the day.'

The cupboards were dark wood and had been well used over the years, judging by the scrapes and stains. Sets of knives and other untensils were ranged along the walls close to marble chopping-blocks. It was all spotlessly clean and although it looked old-fashioned, there were dishwashers, an Aga, and modern freezers—no doubt full of salmon from the river. Arran confirmed it.

'We get rather tired of it, in fact. Guests catch them and we put them on the menu for them—after they've been photographed, of course. Ready?'

She had pulled on a blue woollen beret and now she threw a matching scarf around her neck. She collected her leather boots as they left by the porch and with her hands deep in the pockets of her navy duffel she led the way around the outbuildings.

'This is Shula, my horse,' she said, slipping the mare a titbit.

'That's Hugh's, but he's rarely here to exercise him so we all take a turn.' She moved to the next stable and slapped the black horse's neck, pulled his ears. 'Do you ride, John?'

'I can stay on, just.'

One of the dogs, a black Labrador, joined them, lolloping ahead as they moved on through the trees and on to the open ground beyond. The view was breathtaking, with the hills white-capped and looking deceptively close. There were dark patches of forestry on the lower slopes, but above them the hills were bleak, with gashes of bare rock further up. Arran followed his gaze.

'It's always changing, and beautiful when the heather turns them purple. Now you'll understand why I would never want to sell an inch of this place.'

'Where is the area you are parting with?'

She stopped, and he almost bumped into her, but she stood her ground and pointed. He was so close that he could smell the cleanness of her skin and hair. Maybe it was something to do with living in the fresh country air, but he'd never seen a girl who sparkled quite as much as Arran Sinclair. And it wasn't just her complexion that glowed, but the feeling that every part of her was alive and ready for anything that life could throw at her. It made him feel stale.

He looked in the direction she was indicating.

'Over there. You can't see it because of that high ground and hopefully they won't build high enough to be visible.' She sounded as if she knew it was a vain hope. 'But we'll have the river between us as well.'

They could hear the river and soon they were on the bank. It wasn't a wide river, but it was running pretty full over jagged rocks that just showed their black tips above the surface.

Arran turned to look up at him. 'I've been so bloody angry since you told me how much Hugh will get from the sale.' She kicked at the undergrowth with a boot. 'I have plans, but there's never enough cash. I want to start a fish farm but first I must extend the central heating in the house and get more rooms modernized. And I could do it all with that kind of money.' But as if she couldn't stay angry for long, she grinned. 'Our American guests don't like cold healthy bedrooms.'

They stood for a while looking back at the house which John now noticed had a wing facing them. It gave the place an unbalanced look, as if the original builder had intended a closed quadrangle and had then changed his mind.

'Mother has rooms in that wing and the rest is empty. I'm going to talk her into moving across above the offices so that wing can be just for visitors—that's the next step but it all takes such a long time.'

She sighed and turned back to walk along the river bank, John followed slowly, wondering how much money Carrick had wasted already. Arran continued telling him about her plans, the hope that they could produce venison on a com-

mercial basis as well as the deer-stalking they already pro-
vided for visitors.

It wasn't long before he was numb with cold and Arran
was hugging her coat around her as the first flakes of snow
drifted down. She threw a stick for the dog, apparently
intending to walk even further from the house, but John
had seen enough. He wanted to turn the conversation back
to Hugh Carrick, to make use of every moment he had.

'Has your stepfather never taken any interest in your
plans?'

Arran shook her head. 'Well, at the beginning he might
have. He had consultants in to make a financial projection,
I think. The papers are still around somewhere but he never
did anything that they advised, as far I as can tell.'

'I'd like to take a look at them,' John told her. 'You never
know, they might be of use even now.'

If Carrick had papers of any kind they might be kept
together with others that might reveal more of the man. He
felt his hopes rise.

'I've never studied them,' Arran confessed. 'To be
honest, I wouldn't understand them but if you'd give me
an opinion I'd be grateful. Though you know, I didn't ask
you here for a free consultation,' she went on shyly.

And he did feel a twinge of guilt then because in fact he'd
come to spy and not to do her any favours at all. 'Let's get
back then and see what we can find out,' he said.

'Lunch will be ready. We can talk things over with
McNeil and then I'll leave you to your analysing afterwards. McNeil can tell you all the problems much better
than I can, although with him it's strictly practical details.
He knows we're short of capital and to be honest, he hates
changes. I think he'd work for nothing if it would help and
so would a lot of the men because they've been here all
their lives. That's why Hugh makes me so angry. He
doesn't realize the responsibility of keeping the workers in

jobs. They have families and there isn't anything else in the area for them.'

They were on the way back and now the snow was heavier, blowing directly into their faces. John felt the cold penetrate right to the core of his spine but although that was enough to make him shiver, part of that cold feeling was because this girl knew more about fighting to survive than he did.

They headed straight for the large, warm kitchen that was heated by the stove. McNeil was already there, his cheeks glowing red with the warmth and he'd shed his tweed jacket to show a colourful Fair Isle waistcoat.

'That weather is settling in. You'll no have an easy drive back, I'm thinking.'

'Most of it's motorway,' John reassured him.

'Aye, but not the bit between it and us. We get blocked every time there's a heavy fall.'

Arran looked concerned, but John was determined to see Carrick's papers and he wasn't going to be rushed into leaving without seeing them.

He didn't learn anything useful from McNeil during the meal except that the workforce had been cut back as far as was possible.

'It's a vicious circle, you see,' the man explained. 'To make money you need the staff but then you have a big wage bill. We have people on part-time hours and some work in the house as well as outside—I'm at a loss to see where we can save any more and that's a fact.'

John could have given them a lecture on cost-effectiveness, but until he saw the books . . . and anyway, today there was no time. And he remembered Rees's sadness that the Sinclair estate might be just another in the long list of big estates that were gradually disappearing. It wasn't hopeful for Arran Sinclair and her ambitions to keep the business going.

Arran led him to the floor above after they'd eaten.

'These are Hugh's rooms,' she said, opening a door. 'I'm never in here but they get cleaned if he's bringing friends for a visit.'

'Does he do that often?'

She frowned. 'Lately there have been the same faces but he used to entertain much more. These people—the latest ones—don't like it here, so I don't know why he bothered. Hugh likes riding but they didn't. As far as I could see, they stayed up half the night playing cards and drinking, and to be honest, I stayed well out of their way.'

'Did you actually meet any of them?'

She didn't seem to want to talk about it or even to want to enter Carrick's rooms. She stood in the doorway and looked around with distaste, as if Carrick and his friends were still in occupation.

'I was introduced once. Scott—he was one. A man who owned property or something who was thinking of getting into time-shares. I didn't like him. He didn't say much but . . . he didn't need to—do you know what I mean? He's the only one who came back a few times and he always brought two others, strange men who were like body-guards.' She hesitated. 'They made a sandwich, with him in the middle. And Hugh was different, too, when Scott came with him. My stepfather is not a pleasant man, although he can be very charming when he chooses to be. He's arrogant and has a vile temper and he upsets everyone —even McNeil and he's the most gentle man I know. But when Scott came, Hugh seemed to . . . try to please him. It was disgusting to watch, the way he almost grovelled, and yet he was his usual self with us. I hate him coming here.' That burst out from her and she seemed close to tears. 'So I'll sell the land even if it means we take years to catch up.' Her beautiful eyes stared at him and he was

astounded at the way that she had opened up to him
honestly.

He hardly knew her and yet she trusted him, or perhaps
she just needed someone unconnected with the estate to
listen to her. She was carrying a heavy burden and who
could she turn to? Her mother was a semi-invalid, her
brother had deserted his share of the responsibility, and
McNeil, while supportive, wasn't in any legal sense able to
help her except as a father-figure.

'I can understand that,' John said, 'but I'm a bit worried
about the legal position. You are getting good legal advice?'
He kept his tone even, uninvolved, although he felt he was
becoming more and more involved with the Sinclair family.

She nodded, in control of herself again. 'Oh yes. My
father's lawyer is still a friend.' She edged away. 'The
papers will be in Hugh's desk, I think—come down when
you're ready.'

And she left him to search for the papers himself, feeling
like an intruder as he did so. First he surveyed the room.
Carrick's choice of furniture told him something about the
man and it was obvious that he had furnished these rooms
himself since the rest of the house was so different. The
carpet was pale cream and expensive, the chairs black
leather with smoked glass tables beside each one. The fireplace was Adam style and over it was a large modern print
which on close inspection turned out to be quite erotic. The
desk was under the window and was fully eight feet long,
leather-topped and bare apart from a crystal ashtray. There
was a layer of dust over everything, so Carrick was not
expected in the near future.

It was not a comfortable room and John felt he was
leaving a signature of footprints as he walked across the
carpet. He felt like an intruder in a brothel-keeper's office,
for the rooms had been created to impress and showed no
sign of good taste. He shrugged and started opening the

drawers of the desk before he even looked through the other rooms.

Most were empty, one had an old engagement book that held nothing of interest. Carrick kept his papers somewhere else. John moved to a door that led to a bedroom and without too much of a qualm he opened the bedside cabinet, flicked through some pornographic magazines and then turned to the wardrobes that filled one wall.

There were a lot of clothes in dust-covers, all the pockets empty. Carrick was fussy about his clothes, most still had dry-cleaning tags on them. There were narrow drawers under one lot of hangers but these held socks, ties and monogrammed handkerchiefs. He turned to the shelves, pushed away tweed caps, silk scarves . . . nothing. Next the shoes, neatly stretched on trees and all handmade . . . pushed a hand past the rack and touched a cardboard box. Bingo.

But in it there were just log books for a boat called *Sea Princess* and he idly flicked through them. Carrick's boat was obviously a sea-going job and he liked the west coast of Scotland as well as the Med ports. John noted down some of the anchorages that Carrick used regularly, which included Granton, but had no idea if that information was going to be of much use.

He hit gold under the last log book and he stared at the small packets in his hand with curiosity. In television dramas he'd seen heroin wrapped like this but to see the white powder for real . . . It looked innocuous, like talc, but if Carrick was an addict it explained the explosive moods that Arran described. Carefully he replaced them and continued his search.

There was no sign of the papers that Arran had mentioned; perhaps Carrick had disposed of them. He tried to put everything back as he'd found it and then looked through the other rooms.

Guest bedrooms, amply supplied with drinks, two bath-
rooms all fitted out in flash tiling and gilt fittings, thick
white towels. Carrick had spared no expense on his own
quarters. He went back to the sitting-room and went to the
bookshelves and the cupboards below. He was crouched
down sliding the doors of these open when he became aware
that he was being watched.

An elegant lady in her late fifties stood in the doorway
with one hand supporting herself on the lintel. It was obvious that she was Arran's mother because the likeness was
unmistakable, but although she was tall and slender, she
was also very frail. Her skin looked transparent, stretched
over her bones as if it had been grafted there.

'Who are you and what are you doing in here?' she asked
quietly and with dignity.

CHAPTER 14

John straightened up and tried to smile reassuringly.

'I'm John Leith, an accountant. Your daughter thought there might be papers here—an old analysis of the estate's projected income . . . but I can't find them.'

She smiled graciously and with something close to relief, as if he was an honoured guest she'd forgotten to welcome properly. There was an air of vagueness in her expression, and John could understand why Arran felt protective of her mother. She came forward, moving with care and held out her hand.

'Pleased to meet you, Mr Leith. I'm Lorna Sinclair.' Her flesh was cold, her fingers lacking any grip. 'I think I might have those papers but I can't be sure.' It bothered her and he could see her searching her memory.

'It's not important,' he told her gently, which was probably the truth anyway.

And as they left the room together, he wondered if she had forgotten that her name was no longer Sinclair, but Carrick. Arran had said her mother's rooms were in the other wing, so why was she wandering around in this part of the house? Expecting to find her husband here? Why would she be there if she was afraid of him, as Arran said? He didn't dare ask any of those questions. Instead she allowed him to take her arm and lead her to the descending stairs and it was only when he saw the prepared tea-things that he realized that mother and daughter probably made a point of sharing an after-lunch cup of tea, since Lorna had certainly not appeared for the meal itself.

It was set out in a pleasant little sitting-room where a log fire sent warmth out to every corner. John walked with

Lorna Sinclair to a chair close to the fire and waited until she'd settled herself into it. Although she had leaned on his arm there was no weight to her at all and her loose dress showed that she hadn't always been so painfully thin.

'Thank you,' she said quietly as John stood over her with his back to the fire. Carrick's rooms had not been heated and he was chilled. When Arran came into the room she scolded her mother.

'I could have brought it to your room today.'

'But then I wouldn't have met Mr Leith,' her mother said with a smile. 'He couldn't find what he was looking for, by the way.' And there was a hint of shrewdness in her eyes, as if there was an unspoken conspiracy between the two of them. Did she realize that John had been snooping? He felt more than a touch of admiration for both these women.

'Have you noticed the weather?' Arran asked as she held out a plate of cakes.

John glanced out of the window at the heavy snow that was covering everything like a blanket. he smiled ruefully and shook his head.

'No. I'd better hit the road soon.'

'You didn't find anything, then?' Arran said, glancing over at her mother, but Lorna had retreated into a world of her own and was gazing at the flames in the fireplace. John shook his head.

'I can guess what the papers said.' In fact he could probably draft out accurate copies without doing any more research. The Sinclair estate was doomed unless Arran married a pop star or an oil-rich Arab. She could struggle on for years, slowly losing money while preserving the jobs of her workers, but in the end she would have to sell off more chunks for developers to gobble up until there was nothing left to keep her workers busy. But he hadn't been asked for his opinion and he didn't give it. You didn't tell

people their plans were just dreams . . . Well, sometimes
he had to, but his clients were not usually pretty young
women weighed down with responsibilities.

There was no point in staying any longer. Arran and her
mother had nothing further to tell him except by implication: that Hugh Carrick was a ruthless man who had no
qualms about how he got his income.

'I'll keep in touch about the sale of the land,' he said as
she saw him out by the back porch. He brushed snow from
his windscreen and the rear window and as he drove off he
saw that Arran was still in the doorway. She returned his
wave, and he thought she looked sorry to see him go.

The snow had not had the chance to lie on the motorway
and the drive back to Edinburgh was not all that bad, but
the sky was heavy with the promise of more to come. He
did wonder if he should keep going to Elmwood but decided
to stop at the West End and see if his office had been
properly cleared—not that there was much to be moved
since the fittings belonged to the company who owned the
block.

The late afternoon traffic was a solid jam on the outskirts
of Edinburgh but as he neared his office he was able to take
side streets and then stepped out of the car into slush. His
rooms were indeed bare. There were marks on the carpet
where his filing cabinets had stood and the desk drawers
hung open, empty. Only his old print of the Forth Bridge
hung on the wall, and he realized he had never bothered
to personalize the place. He had been stepping carefully
around the newest stain on the carpet, made by his own
blood, and it had darkened to a dirty brown. Someone still
had to pay for that.

He had mixed feelings about leaving because once his
wife had perched on the desk and she used to bring in fresh
flowers to brighten the place up. They'd made plans in this

room, that he wouldn't be in rented accommodation long, that one day he would be the busiest accountant in Edinburgh . . .

'Sorry, love, I forgot the dreams,' he murmured. He reached out and took down the print and it left a dark rectangle on the wall. Tucking it under his arm, he checked the phone and found it still connected, so he rang Tollis and told him what he'd found in Carrick's wardrobe.

'Heroin. That makes it worthwhile having another look at Carrick. Pity you couldn't have pinched a sample,' Tollis said. 'Anyway, I'll pass that on to Jamieson.'

'You might check a man called Scott as well. He's been up there looking over that land. Arran says he's in property, interested in time-shares.'

Tollis snorted. 'For property read casinos. His name crops up every time we take a look at Carrick.'

'Anyway, Carrick is not welcome at the estate and they don't know when he's coming back.'

'Are you coming here tonight?'

'No, with the weather closing in I think I'll head for Elmwood and see how David is doing.'

He made a few other calls and in half an hour he was leaving the city once more but in the opposite direction.

He followed the coast road, with the sea on his left. Snow was falling heavily and he drove carefully but there wasn't much traffic on the road. Finding the heroin had inched him nearer to the truth and for the first time in a week he felt that he was no longer helpless. If only they could find definite proof that Hugh Carrick was behind the assaults, he would at least know who the enemy was. He would have a face.

Tollis had said nothing about the Grey brothers. Where were they now, he wondered. Frightened to death no doubt, and keeping their heads down. It was strange to think that in Edinburgh where ordinary people went about their lives, there was this other element that rarely surfaced. You could walk along streets and bump into people like the Grey brothers and not know what they did.

He hadn't been paying attention to following traffic but now he glanced in his mirror and saw a red Fiesta behind him. Hadn't it been there when he left the city? He was seeing criminals in his dreams as well and he couldn't live like this, looking over his shoulder all the time.

He slowed but the other car made no attempt to overtake. It was quite dark now and the blizzard made visibility poor. Soon he saw only its headlights which stayed at exactly the same distance no matter how he speeded up or slowed. A lorry passed both of them, sending up slush and grit, the driver going as if he had radar in his cab, but the Fiesta stayed put.

It was probably an old lady driver, caught out in bad conditions, keeping on his tail for reassurance. So much for his brave new image, but all the same he was uneasy and kept an eye on it in his mirror. He left the main road at the turn-off for Elmwood and then watched to see what the Fiesta did. Its headlights swung around the corner and took up the same position behind him again, not close enough for him to see who was driving. Damn it to hell, he would be at the gates of Elmwood soon—was the car going to follow him right up the drive? This side road had not had the benefit of traffic to clear the snow and his were the only tracks in the virgin layer; the hedgerows on top of each rising verge were white humps in his headlights.

There was barely room for the other car to pass, but the driver showed no sign of wanting to anyway. The only place the other car could be going was to the farm at the end of the track. John realized his hands were gripping the steering-wheel very tightly as he peered ahead looking for Elmwood's gates.

Then he heard a zipping sound close to his left ear. A

round hole punctured the rear windscreen and the rest was opaque and ready to fall out. Only a bullet could have caused that and he could no longer see the following car, or what its occupants were doing. He reached into the glove compartment and then twisted quickly and hurled an aerosol can at the back window, knocking most of the glass away. Now he could see but, stupidly, he felt naked without its protection. He tried to swallow but his mouth was bone dry. He looked back to see if more shots were going to follow but he was blinded by the headlights behind and the snow being sucked in through the gap. The other car was much closer, so he put his foot down hard on the accelerator.

The Fiesta was edging up beside him, both cars careering dangerously down the narrow road and there was no room for errors. Not that it mattered, because whoever had fired the shot was intent on getting close enough to do it again. In desperation and with no skill, John turned the wheel sharply and felt the shock of the collision as he rammed the other car.

It shouldn't have done more than dissuade the other driver but for some freakish reason it sent the Fiesta heading straight up the verge and the bank beyond. He caught a quick impression of the other car running up the bank as if it was a ramp, then it was out of his line of vision.

He glanced back through the hole where the rear window had been and saw the Fiesta do a graceful roll over the hedge into the field. He clenched his jaw and kept going.

He was in the drive two minutes later and without pausing to shut the car door he ran into the house, used the phone on the hall table, and ignored Janet as she came to see why the front door was wide open.

'Can you put me through to Chief Inspector Robert Jamieson, police headquarters in Edinburgh—it's an emergency.'

He brushed snow from his hair and face while he waited and tried to ignore the trembling of his hands. They'd fired at him and it was no longer a question of searching, but of killing.

'Who is calling, please? Chief Inspector Jamieson is busy at the moment.' A female voice asked for details that he hadn't the time to give.

'Tell him it's John Leith and I need to speak to him now.'

Another wait and Janet was gently closing the door and standing anxiously looking at him. It was more than likely that over the years she had learned something about Rees's work, and that there had been other emergencies in the past. She probably knew more about that than Rees had ever told him. He could hear background voices that included Jamieson's calm tones. The phone was picked up at the other end.

'Mr Leith?'

His voice was steady and reassuring and John felt relief flood over him. He took a deep breath and tried to relate what had happened in as few words as possible. 'Inspector, my car was followed—I was on my way to my uncle's home, Elmwood. The driver shot at me.'

'Where are you now?' This time the tone was businesslike.

'I'm in Rees's house, Elmwood. I hit the other car and it went over a ditch into a field. The driver is probably hurt.' Not that he gave a damn about that—he hoped he'd broken his neck.

'Stay where you are. I'll see to it.'

Jamieson hung up and left John with the dialling tone buzzing in his ear. He put the phone down slowly. How long would it take for someone to arrive? And in the meantime would someone from that car be able to come up to Elmwood? . . . He walked quickly to the sitting-room where he would have a clear view of the drive, but there was a

blizzard raging and he couldn't see ten feet. Janet had followed him, her face tense, hands clasped.

'Where is everyone?'

Janet wasn't flustered. 'Rees was tired and he went up
to take a nap. David's in the kitchen with the puppy.
Gwen's at the village shops.'

She didn't ask what was going on because no doubt she'd
heard enough of what he'd told Jamieson. John blessed her
for not making a fuss.

'Stay with David. I have to go and keep an eye on who
comes up the drive.' He managed to smile at her. 'Don't
worry, I'll run back like hell if anyone appears. Don't bother
Rees with this,' he added, and she nodded.

Later he was to remember that he'd taken the time to lift
a waterproof jacket from a hook in the cloakroom. That
had been automatic, because his mind certainly wasn't concerned with getting wet. He also took a heavy walking stick
and hoped that he wouldn't need to use it, and then he
waited for what seemed an age down near the gates. He
stood in the lee of a stone pillar and listened for the cars,
but there wasn't a sound. From time to time he peered up
the road to where the other car had crashed, but there was
no sign of anyone walking from that spot. It was eerie, with
the snow falling like a blanket all around him and it even
cut him off from the house. His feet went numb with cold
and he shuffled them. Snow went down his neck, stuck to
his eyes, went into his mouth, but all the time his ears
strained for the sound of Jamieson's car. Were the occupants of the Fiesta trapped in their upturned car? He pictured them struggling to get free, sneaking towards him in
the blizzard, and then he heard vehicles approaching and
saw the flash of a blue lamp.

He had never been so pleased to see another human being
in his life as when he saw Jamieson step from the leading
car.

'Get in and show us where this happened, Mr Leith.'
Jamieson was courteous but to the point, and John knew it
was intended to have a calming effect.

'We can walk,' he said. 'It's just back here a bit.'

He led the way and other officers got out of cars and
followed. An ambulance was in the line too with men in
orange plastic jackets jumping down to join the procession.

The marks where the car had left the road were already
almost hidden by the snow. John pointed them out and
then watched as policemen ploughed up the bank. Two
vaulted over the top and the rest waited in silence until a
face reappeared.

'You'd better see this, sir. You're never going to believe
it, though.'

That was enough to make everyone curious and Jamieson
made no objection to them all going to look, John included.
The other car was on its roof but it couldn't have chosen a
worse spot to land. The farmer must have been using a
digger vehicle to clear the ditch and the Fiesta had landed
smack on top of the digger's great claws. They had impaled
the car and the men as well, still held by their seat-belts.

John didn't go any closer after that first look and some
of the policemen were a bit squeamish and turned their
heads away. Jamieson peered into the depths and then
crouched down. He didn't say anything, but straightened,
came back to where John stood and with a nod of his head
indicated that he'd seen enough.

'We'll have a chat in the warmth of the house. Your car
up there, is it?'

John nodded. He felt drained. They didn't say anything
at all until they reached his car and Jamieson walked right
round it before joining him on the steps at the door. The
policeman's mouth was compressed as they stepped inside.

'My uncle isn't too well. Janet says he's resting, so if
possible I don't want him disturbed,' John said and

Jamieson nodded. He took off his coat, handed it over and then looked around the hall until John joined him.

'Nice house,' he said, almost to himself, and then followed John into the sitting-room where a fire was lit. It was so normal, so comfortable, that it seemed unreal and as if the Inspector was used to dealing with this sort of situation he looked around for the drinks cabinet. Without asking, he poured two Scotches and handed one to John.

'Sit you down now and tell me all about it,' he said. He was just like a nice doctor come to discuss troublesome symptoms, only he didn't have a bag with a cure in it.

John sat down and drained his glass and let the whisky go all the way down before he prepared to tell all. Jamieson waited patiently as if nothing in the world was surprising any more.

CHAPTER 15

'I noticed the car behind me when I was on the coast road,' he said.

Jamieson nodded, as if it was perfectly normal for a driver to be worried about being followed and John felt like laughing.

The policeman leaned forward. 'At that point could you see the men in it?'

John shook his head. 'The snow blotted everything out and I wasn't sure it was following me, not even when it turned off the main road behind me—it could have been going to the farm.'

Jamieson accepted that. 'You had a look in the car— not a pleasant sight—but did you recognize them?' His eyebrows went up with the question but his calm manner made it sound a reasonable thing to ask when in fact what he meant was, 'Did you manage to ignore the blood and gore and get a look at their faces?'

John hadn't wanted to see what the claws had done to them but in the few seconds that he'd looked in the shattered car's windows, his mind had registered very clearly the expressions on their faces. Lips drawn back in grimaces of horror, eyes wide open and staring. They were not the features of men but images from a horror movie, too unreal to recognize. 'The one in that photograph you showed me,' he said before getting up to re-fill his glass.

Jamieson sat further back in his chair. 'We had a very strange piece of information—that's not quite right, I suppose,' and for a moment he looked amused. 'In fact, it would be more accurate to say we got information from a

strange source. From your father-in-law, Albert Gumley.'
He let that sink in before going on. 'He told us that Joe and
Henry Grey had been at the root of most of your troubles
—we knew that, of course, and it's a pity we didn't find
them before this happened. They might have told us a lot
more. But they've never used guns before. They're not the
type and that's what's hard to understand.' Jamieson
blinked, lost in thought, as if puzzling over what could have
turned two such villains into killers. John was thinking
much the same thing.

'We'll take your car away with theirs and get rid of the
other detritus in due course. It's a very interesting case.
Especially since you found drugs at the Sinclair place. Why
did you suspect Carrick at all?'

'I don't know,' John said wearily. 'His name was in the
files I had with me . . .'

Jamieson interrupted gently. 'On the night you were
pushed off the road?' He stared blandly at John's discomfort. 'I read the signs the next morning,' he said.

John drew in a deep breath. 'Yes, well, Carrick's file was
not important but his was the only name in the bunch that
had any possible connection with shady dealings. I had a
feeling about him,' he finished lamely.

'The amateur's hunch,' Jamieson said drily. 'Well, now
that we've had him brought to our attention, we'll keep an
eye open for him.' He stood up and moved towards the
door and then suddenly spun back to face John. 'I'd advise
you to be very careful, of course. Make no mistake, Mr
Leith, you're in very great danger.'

'But why?' John burst out. 'That's what I want to
know.'

Jamieson didn't look too concerned, just puzzled.

'So do I, Mr Leith. So do I.'

Out in the hall again, Rees was coming slowly down the
stairs, leaning on the banister rail, and he stopped in his

tracks when he saw Jamieson. The policeman paused too, and his sharp eyes took in Rees's grey colour. 'I'm just leaving, Mr Kramer. Your nephew will put you in the picture.'

He took his coat from John and put his hands in the pockets without fastening it up. 'I'll be in touch—I'll see myself out.'

John waited for Rees to join him and followed his uncle into the sitting-room, saw him settled and then went back to the drinks cabinet to pour a Scotch for him, but Rees declined.

'I sent for Jamieson,' John said quietly. He sat opposite his uncle and told him the whole story because he knew that nothing else that would satisfy Rees. Rees took it in and shook his head from time to time, but by the time John had finished, he looked so awful that John wished that his uncle had stayed in his room and therefore would have missed the whole thing.

'Rees, have you seen a doctor?'

Rees shook his head but didn't protest when John said he was going to send for one.

'But first I'll see you upstairs.'

Rees let John undress him and then lay down as if unutterably tired. His face looked so drawn that John went right to the phone to call out the GP an old friend of his uncle who would stand no nonsense.

He was there in five minutes, kicking snow from his shoes before going upstairs. John explained his anxiety, then went to fetch Janet who was about to supervise David's bath.

'I'll take over—see what the doctor thinks.'

David knew nothing of what had happened or that the police cars were still parked on the road, but Gwen arrived shortly after and she was full of questions.

'And the doctor's car is outside.'

'I'll explain later. Rees isn't well.'

He ran David's bath and let the boy fill it with plastic boats but drew the line at the dog coming to spectate. Then he gathered up his son's discarded clothes. It was a moment of saneness in a world gone mad.

Within the hour Rees was in hospital and John stayed in the waiting-room while the doctors examined him. It was nearly midnight before he was told of his uncle's condition.

'The ECG is showing evidence of a recent heart attack. He's being moved to the Coronary Care Unit.'

John was allowed to see Rees for a few moments; there were electrodes on his chest and a machine beeping with every beat of his heart. 'Sorry, John, it was all for the best,' he said weakly.

'Of course. This is the best place to be for a few days,' he said before he slipped out to phone Janet, who would certainly be awake and waiting for his call.

'I'm leaving here now but I'll stay in town tonight,' he said. 'I'll phone you again in the morning.' And as he hung up, he knew that Janet was unlikely to sleep that night.

In her late fifties, Janet had been Rees's housekeeper for over twenty years and he'd often wondered why she and Rees didn't marry since he was certain that all that was lacking was a certificate joining them legally.

He walked from the Royal Infirmary to the Sentinel Office which was five minutes away and, as he'd expected, there was still a light showing in Tollis's room.

'What's up?'

'Rees had another heart attack. He's in intensive care, but stable so far.'

John threw off his coat wearily and dropped into a chair while Tollis poured out a mug of coffee for him from the jug that permanently steamed on a hotplate. 'And the police have my car so you're stuck with me for tonight.'

Tollis paused as he was handing John the mug and John told him the latest about the death of the Grey brothers. Tollis whistled and then looked grim.

'Jamieson came down himself,' John said, 'but he doesn't give much away. I haven't a clue what he's doing about all this.'

They talked into the night, until John was too tired to think straight and then he wrapped himself in a blanket and stretched himself between two chairs to sleep. He borrowed Tollis's razor in the grey morning and phoned the infirmary, where a nurse confirmed that Rees's condition was unchanged. She advised him not to visit until after the doctors had made their rounds in the morning. He and Tollis snatched a quick breakfast and then a call came in that had Tollis on his feet and full of energy again.

'Carrick's in town—sheer luck he was spotted and I've got a couple of men on his tail. I want to see him for myself and you'd better come too—at least then I'll know where you are,' he said drily.

'I thought you weren't convinced he was involved?'

'I'm keeping my options open and I just want to know what the bastard's here for.'

Carrick was staying in a hotel in Princes Street, so Tollis and John took over from the two men who had been watching him and that meant strolling up and down in Princes Street gardens. It was freezing. Melting snow dripped from the trees and the only other living things brave enough to be there were the pigeons.

'Aren't we a bit conspicuous?' John asked, and Tollis merely shrugged.

'The other two will be back when they've picked up their car and then we'll go into the lounge. Carrick's with a girl

and I want to get a look at her, too. The coffee lounge is
opposite the reception desk so we'll be able to see them if
they decide to leave.'

It was a boring and bleak fifteen minutes before
Tollis's men returned. One hopped out of the car to
report.

'Carrick is in Room ninety-five. He's asked for a hired
car but there's no word on how he got here—could have
come from Glasgow. And he's checking out this morning.'

That man stayed in the gardens, the other stayed with
the car, ready to move on if a traffic warden appeared—
John didn't envy them but suspected they were used to
such work, then he and Tollis left the snowy paths of the
gardens to the pigeons.

They climbed the stairs to the coffee lounge where there
was a glass partition giving a clear view of the reception
desk and the lifts. John had his back to this but he knew
the instant that Carrick came from the lift because of the
change of expression in Tollis's eyes.

'That's him,' Tollis muttered, and John looked through
the glass at Hugh Carrick. He was tall, with close-cropped
hair that was silver—the sort of head of hair that never
goes bald. His skin was tanned and that alone made him
stand out against the pale winter complexions of the other
guests, but Carrick would have stood out anyway because
of his clothes and his demeanour. He moved like an athlete
and he was arrogant. Standing with his overcoat thrown
loosely over his shoulders, he looked on impatiently as his
bill was made out. The heavy gold jewellery on wrists and
fingers, the cut of his suit, all pointed to a man who would
walk through a gathering, never around it. And all the time
his pale blue eyes were scanning those about him. John and
Tollis were only five feet from him but his presence was
almost tangible. For an instant his eyes settled on Tollis
and then John, but his glance passed on without interest.

The girl with him was like a model, blonde and slender; she too liked expensive jewellery but hers flashed with the fire of real diamonds. John noticed that others were staring and Carrick was aware of the attention he was getting. The man sought it and relished it.

'Don't stare,' Tollis said. 'You're not likely to forget him, are you?'

But John was wondering why Carrick was in Edinburgh and did it mean he was heading for Kramer's to see Rees about the sale of the land, or was he going to the estate? He didn't think Carrick would have any twinge of conscience about taking the girl to the house where his wife was still in residence.

'I'll let our boys know he's leaving.' Tollis got up and strolled to the wide windows that gave guests a panoramic view of the Castle and gardens. He looked out but gave no visible signal—no doubt the men across the street would know exactly what to do next. Carrick was signing a cheque with a flourish of a gold pen and the girl waited patiently. She was beautiful, but it was a practised beauty; her face was hard and in other clothes and another setting she could be a street-walker.

They left, going down the curving staircase to the street entrance, Carrick carrying one small case which gave no clues to his destination because the man had wardrobes full of clothes at the estate.

'My guess is that he's heading up to the estate,' Tollis agreed. 'I'd love to be a fly on the wall when he gets there.'

He made a stop at the desk but Carrick had signed himself and the girl in as a married couple so they still didn't know her name. 'Let's get back, then. Now we have to wait to see what develops.'

But in fact they didn't have to wait long. John was in Rees's office checking up on the day-to-day business and wondering if Carrick would get in touch about the sale; Rees was still in intensive care but if he continued to make progress, he would be moved to a ward the next day. Then Tollis rang and asked if he could come down to the Sentinel office.

'Jamieson just phoned to say that a body has been found. It sounds like Toby.'

CHAPTER 16

John walked through the large working office of Sentinel on his way to Tollis's room and it was obvious that the word had got round. The atmosphere was electric yet quiet. No one was working. Men who happened to be in were standing in groups talking quietly, and their eyes followed him as if in hope that he came with more news.

Mike Cairns was in Tollis's office, slumped in a chair, his eyes staring straight ahead and he didn't seem to notice John enter the room. Tollis was at the window with a cigarette burning his fingers and he turned and looked at John with a set expression that was difficult to read. He had been expecting the worst possible news and now that it had arrived he still seemed numbed by it. He stubbed out the cigarette and lit another while John waited to see what they were to do next. He didn't speak to Mike because he didn't know what to say.

Tollis broke the silence and as he spoke, Mike's head came round to face him. 'Jamieson wants an identification of the body and I've been trying to persuade Mike to let me go.'

Mike stirred and spoke as if his mouth was unbearably dry or perhaps his words were slurred with shock. 'And I told him I'll see for myself . . . I'd rather have John go with me.'

John flinched and glanced at Tollis, who shook his head and gave an almost imperceptible shrug of his shoulders. He had known that Mike was going to suggest it and he wanted John to go along with it.

'Of course I will,' John said. He didn't know Mike all that well and had never met his son but he still felt very sorry for the man. Tollis took a bottle of Scotch from a drawer and set three chunky glasses carefully amid the chaos on his desk. He poured generous measures in all three and then carried one to Mike.

Mike didn't argue but drank it back in one gulp and then stood up as John swallowed his. 'Let's get on with it,' he said and led the way through the outer office, but Tollis grabbed John's arm and held him back for a moment.

'That body's not going to be a pretty sight. Even in this cold weather there's bound to be some deterioration. If Jamieson agrees, do it by Toby's belongings—Mike knows the procedure but I don't know if he'll agree.' He held John's arm for a second or two longer and John knew that he would have preferred to do this himself to save Mike the ordeal. 'Take him to a quiet pub afterwards if you can. He won't want to come back here and I don't want him to be left on his own . . . there isn't anyone else at home for him.'

John nodded and then swung after Mike who had marched right through the office, past the other men as if he didn't see them. Their expressions were mixed. Mostly John saw pity on their faces, but on others there was anger, and as he followed Mike down to the car he was already wishing it was over. He didn't think Jamieson would expect him to have anything to do with the identification, but maybe Mike would want him there. And that was when his stomach began to feel queasy.

They went in the car he'd been using from the pool but Mike automatically slid behind the wheel and before he started it up, he turned to John. 'Thanks for coming along. It had to be someone . . . not involved with Sentinel—you know what I mean? Not Tollis, not any of the others.' He spoke quietly and the shock was gone from his eyes now. He was resigned to seeing his son lying dead in the mortuary and John supposed that knowing was better than the awful waiting for definite news.

They didn't have far to drive. 'It's in the Cowgate,' Mike said as he spun the wheel at a busy junction.

'Yes, I've been there before,' John said, and Mike's head jerked around to face him for an instant before he had to concentrate on driving again.

'Sorry, I forgot about your wife,' he muttered. 'Stupid of me, maybe you'd rather not come,' he went on, but John shook his head. Now that he was committed he really did want to give Mike all the support he could.

'It's OK,' he assured the big man beside him.

'Maybe it's just as well,' Mike said absently. 'Tollis seems to think you'll work for Sentinel and this sort of thing goes with the job. A lot of the people we're asked to trace have a habit of turning up in that place.' There was no answer to that. And then they were pulling up at the mortuary. It was a fairly modern building set in among much older ones, in a shabby street that ran below the level of one of Edinburgh's famous bridges. John raised his eyes to the traffic crossing the bridge—that was where the real world was but down here was the furtive side of the city, where bodies arrived to be dissected and inspected and the people passing by probably never noticed the discreet sign on the wall.

Mike had to press a bell to be admitted.

'I'm meeting Chief Inspector Jamieson here,' he told the attendant, who showed them into a small waiting-room.

It had chrome chairs with puce-coloured seats, a brown carpet, magazines on a table and a fan heater that made the room far too hot. Neither of them sat down and the attendant told them that Jamieson had not yet arrived.

'I never get used to this place,' Mike said as he lit a cigarette and almost immediately stubbed it out again in a tin ashtray on the table. He fidgeted with his coat buttons, as if he wanted to take the coat off but hoped they wouldn't be there long enough for that. 'You know, they do over a

thousand PMs a year in here. Can you imagine the grief
that causes to lots of people? They showed me a bag of
bones that some workmen had dug up—they have to check
in case they're the result of a crime.'

Nerves were making him talk as if they were in a dentist's
waiting-room and his eyes kept darting to the door.

'Where the hell is Jamieson?' he said at last, going to the
door to look into the long corridor just as John heard the
sound of footsteps approaching. 'About time,' Mike muttered, going to meet the policeman. John followed slowly
and watched the two men meet and confer and as he got
near he heard Jamieson say, 'I thought Tollis would do
this, so I said they could keep the body on the table. The
pathologist is keen to get started . . .' He turned to John
and explained, 'Usually for relatives they use the little room
over there,' and through the open door John could see a
trestle table draped with a purple cloth edged with gold
braid. He'd seen that before too.

Jamieson looked put out, indecisive, but Mike made the
decision for him.

'It's all right, I don't mind about the niceties. Just let me
see my son.'

Jamieson shrugged and led the way back the way he had
come. They passed through a room which had refrigeration
units along one wall and John noted they were numbered
up to 36. Then they were in the dissecting room where there
were two steel tables, sinks, and a glass viewing room at
one end with a row of green wellington boots under it. One
steel table was empty and it had drainage holes along its
length. The other held a body covered with a white sheet.
There was a strong smell that caught at John's throat.

He was behind Mike and Jamieson and he kept his eyes
on their backs, saw Jamieson pause and look up at the taller
man. His hand hovered at Mike's elbow but didn't actually
touch him. Mike stepped forward and lifted the sheet him-

self but John couldn't see what he saw. He was watching Mike, wishing that a doctor was present instead of the attendant who was obviously waiting to prepare for the arrival of the pathologist.

Mike seemed to hold the sheet aloft for an age, his back rigid, but then a sound like a sob came from his throat and he turned away. In that instant John saw what Mike had seen and his stomach heaved and he had to swallow hard. Then Jamieson quickly replaced the sheet and ushered Mike away.

John didn't remember walking back to the hot waiting-room but suddenly Jamieson had a hip flask out of his pocket and they all got a mouthful of a good malt. He didn't ask Mike to confirm verbally that he'd just seen his dead son. There was no need. Mike was ashen and his hands trembled as he handed back the flask.

'He was shot,' Mike said as if stunned. Jamieson was frowning, jaw clenched tight, but he was confirming that it was a fact. 'Who found him and where?' Mike demanded.

'A farmer, when he was putting out feed for his sheep. He was in a ditch.'

'In a ditch. Christ.' Mike's voice broke. There was nothing anyone could say. John could still taste the smell of the dissecting room in his mouth and he was desperate for fresh air but he didn't move until Mike began to make for the door.

'Are you staying with him?' Jamieson asked and John nodded.

'Then let him get drunk if that's what it takes.'

But Mike couldn't get drunk although he downed whisky after whisky. And after a while he wanted to go home, but they'd left the car near the mortuary and had to flag down a taxi. At the door of his house in the north end of the city Mike insisted that John had done his bit and that now he should get off home to his own bed.

'I need to be on my own for a bit anyway.'

'I'd like a coffee before I go,' John said mildly. And Mike agreed to that and to having some himself. And the night passed with the two of them sleeping in the living-room of the comfortable little house which a son would never again share with his father. It was easily one of the worst nights in John's life.

CHAPTER 17

Church bells woke John that Sunday morning but by then Mike was sober and the big man was suffering from a hangover that made him blunder towards the bathroom where he was noisily sick.

'Get the fuck out of here,' he shouted when John tried to help, then reached for a bottle again. That at least John could understand but he wished he had Tollis's knack of talking and calming. In the end he phoned Tollis when Mike was paying a repeat visit to the bathroom.

'I don't want to leave him,' he said, 'but I'm not much use either.'

'Tell him I need him here looking smart and ready for work,' Tollis said sharply. 'You can't stop him hurting but I know Mike and he'll be better if he's busy. I'll send a car.' And like magic his instruction worked. Mike showered and shaved and although he looked like death warmed up, he was docile when the car arrived.

John left him to Tollis's care and went up to Rees's flat where he cleaned himself up and shaved.

His eyes felt gritty and his body protested from two nights sleeping in chairs, but he was full of guilty relief to be away from Mike's grief. He phoned the Royal to see how Rees was and was told he'd had a good night. One thing was sure: Rees could not be told yet about Toby.

He was at a loose end. Rees's business was running itself and the finance department had taken over his own clients temporarily. Everything seemed suspended. A body had been found but they had made no progress at all. His father-in-law hadn't been in touch and Jamieson was keeping his own investigations private. Was anyone doing anything?

He walked around the empty office suite and ended up in Rees's office where he ran his fingers over the desk that his uncle had used for so many years. Would Rees ever sit behind it again? Restlessly he went to stand by the window and watched sleet slanting across the rooftops, driving into the faces of people going to church. And suddenly he desperately wanted to hear Clare's voice, but as he reached for the phone he remembered that she wouldn't arrive back from Sunningdale until evening. She would be appalled when she heard about Toby . . .

It was a relief when the phone rang and he heard Tollis's voice at the other end. 'Carrick went to the estate as we thought he would, with girlfriend in tow. He's got a nerve. My boys can't keep a proper watch on him there but they're staying close by. You could give Arran a ring and ask her to tip us on when he's leaving.'

'Will do.' But Arran was not available. A young office girl told him she was out and he assumed she meant out on the estate somewhere.

'Can I take a message?'

'No—I'll call back later.' She hadn't asked his name and he didn't volunteer it. As an afterthought he asked if Mr Carrick was in.

'No, he's out too,' she said doubtfully, as if not sure how to handle such an inquiry.

John hung up and rang Tollis. 'He's there, but out. I'll give Arran a ring later on.'

'We do have one piece of information,' Tollis said. 'Carrick's girl is local—or at least she has a flat here in Edinburgh. We'll have a look at her place while she's away.'

'Break in, you mean?'

'Nothing so crude. Our firm services the alarms in that

block. We'll simply do our annual service, but I doubt if we'll find anything.'

'And that's why you want Arran to let you know when Carrick leaves?'

'Mm. He might come back to Edinburgh to stay with the girl. It's . . .' Tollis sighed. 'It's a detail, probably not important, but just sometimes the small things can add up and mean something. We don't know what else to do except cover all the angles. And we've got a more recent photograph of Toby to issue to the press. The men have been passing some out with no feedback, so now we go public. It will be in tomorrow's *Evening News*.'

John had not seen any of the photographs, but perhaps if he took a look it might clear his memory of the gruesome glimpse he'd had of the young man in the mortuary.

'Want to look over the girl's place with me?' Tollis asked, and before John could answer he went on, 'Meet you in the car park in ten minutes.'

The flat was in Rutland Square, not all that far from John's West End office, and was in the same type of Georgian building. Here, though, some of the blocks had been converted into flats and since such properties were wildly expensive, the developers had capitalized by making the flats tiny. The sitting-room and bedroom would be crowded with two people inside, while the bathroom and kitchen were little more than cupboards. Compact was an understatement.

'Won't take long to look this over, will it?' Tollis said, looking around. 'I'll take the bedroom.'

There wasn't room for much in the way of furniture but what there was, was expensive. Sleek B. & O. gear with a selection of compact discs and LPs stood under a . . . John looked closer, and yes, it really *was* a Hockney. He looked around and couldn't see anywhere to keep papers. The flat didn't have the feel of being anyone's home, but was more a *pied-à-terre* that someone like Carrick would use in an emergency.

He ran his hands under the seat cushions of the chairs but found only crumbs. The girl was no housewife. Tollis agreed with his conclusions.

'She lives somewhere else—this is a little love-nest. The bed fills the bedroom and there're only a couple of changes of clothing but at least she believes in putting her name inside her gowns. Jane Freeman. There are only basic toiletries in the bathroom and that stove never saw a saucepan. Let's go.'

In the car, Tollis filled John in on what they'd discovered about Carrick's friend Scott. 'Owner of nightclubs and now looking over the leisure industry. He's a bad one, suspected of gangland killings.' Tollis was silent for a while and then he glanced quickly over at John. 'You know, I've never understood why Carrick hasn't pushed Rees to get that land sold. If he's so desperate for the cash, why isn't he banging on Kramer's door demanding action?'

'Arran thought he was after more than she was prepared to give him.'

Tollis grimaced. 'Don't you think it likely that his good friend Tony Scott might have something to do with it? I wonder if he'll appear on the horizon this trip?' Tollis seemed to be thinking aloud but suddenly he came out of his speculation and shrugged. 'Not that it has anything to do with us. I think Miss Sinclair will have her hands full, though, and I just hope she has good legal backing.'

They pulled in behind the Kramer building but did not go inside. Instead, they walked further down the High Street to a favourite Italian restaurant where Tollis built up his carbohydrate reserves without seeming to taste a bite. And as they walked to the office block he became quiet, as if the problems awaiting him there were already weighing heavily.

'I've got a reporter coming for the details about Toby. I'll have to get the photographs and a statement ready. I suppose it'll just be a "Have you seen this man" type of thing, but Mike won't enjoy seeing that splashed all over the paper tomorrow. It's a helluva business, John.'

Wearily he pushed open the door with its discreet plaque naming the Sentinel office and John followed him up the stairs. Tollis as usual reached for the coffee-pot, but the liquid was over-strong and bitter for John, who refused a cup.

Instead, he reached out and opened a folder that held the photographs of Toby. They were 8 × 10 enlargements, sharp black and white studies of head and shoulders. There were sparkles of happiness in the young man's eyes, as if he was smiling at his best girl. His dark hair was short, he had neat ears and a wide grin, only he didn't look like that any more.

John's mouth was suddenly dry.

'You never met Toby, did you?' Tollis said quietly.

'But I did,' John said, unable to take his eyes from the enlargement. He felt anger welling up, and when he spoke he had a job to control it.

'Why the hell didn't someone show me a picture of Toby? If the men were dishing them out in the streets didn't you think *I* might be interested?' He picked up the photograph again, but he was seeing the bloated object that Mike had had to identify. He felt sick but anger overcame the nausea.

'We've been looking for some connection and it was staring me in the face, only I couldn't work it out because I didn't know who Toby was.'

Tollis had come from behind the desk, his face like thunder. 'Just what the hell are you on about? Sit on your backside and tell me what you mean.'

John didn't move but stayed eye-to-eye with Tollis, their faces only a foot apart.

'I'm talking about the break-in at my flat and my office, about young Tracy getting hurt, everything. It's all to do with Toby's death—it must be.'

'How do you work that out?' Tollis said evenly.

But John just stared back at him, his anger giving way to despair. 'Christ, Tollis, half of it need never have happened,' he said huskily.

'That I'd like to judge for myself but you still haven't told me what you mean. Let's sit down, have a Scotch and talk. Right?'

But John couldn't take his eyes from the smiling photograph. 'It wouldn't have made any difference to him anyway,' he said. He took the chunky glass and then dropped wearily into a chair.

'I did meet Toby only I hadn't a clue who he was. It was on the morning that it all began, before I left for work. I was bringing my suitcase down from the flat to put it in the boot of the car and I had David's birthday present in a carrier and my briefcase . . . and I slipped and dropped the lot. He, Toby, appeared out of nowhere and helped me pick them up. He even put some of it in the car for me.'

'Are you absolutely certain it was Toby?'

'Yes. I asked if I could give him a lift but he looked . . . I don't know . . . edgy. He said thanks, but he was going to buy a paper and read it in a café while he ate breakfast. He looked rough and I thought he was a night worker or something—he hadn't shaved—and he was looking around as if trying to spot someone he knew.'

Tollis blew out his cheeks and then slumped in his seat. He chewed his lip while John's eyes strayed again to the photograph. He couldn't believe that the cheerful young man was dead, was that waxen body he'd caught a glimpse of in the mortuary.

'He must have known he was being followed and he slipped you something. It's the only explanation why they turned their attention to you after they discovered that Toby no longer had it. By God, John, you'd be dead too if they'd found what they wanted.'

'Don't go back to square one, for Christ's sake. Toby gave me nothing and when I reached Gwen's I didn't have anything that I didn't start out with.'

'He must have.' Tollis was emphatic. 'It could be very small, something easily slipped into your pocket or your luggage. Something as small as a key that could have been lost in that first accident, or a piece of paper that is now a soggy mess somewhere.' Tollis's tone was more reasonable and John admitted at last that he could be right.

'But that means it's gone forever.'

'Maybe. But he had information that he wanted to pass to us in Sentinel, because you can be sure that Toby knew who you were. Rees Kramer's nephew is known to everyone by sight. He was in your neighbourhood and saw you coming out of your flat. He must have known he was being followed and you were the nearest help he could reach.'

'Then why didn't he come with me? If he'd just told me, I could have driven him straight here.'

'That's easy to say with hindsight, but he was new to the firm and maybe didn't realize the danger. Who knows? It would be like an adventure and he may have thought he was free and clear and nobody would be the wiser . . . But I wonder what the hell he found out that made him take the chance. I don't suppose you noticed anyone else that morning?'

John shook his head. 'You think that whoever was after Toby followed me?'

'Must have. That means there were at least two of them and both had cars—one to go after you, the other to get hold of Toby. I wonder how they got him into a car, what reason they gave?' Tollis was thinking again. 'They wouldn't risk violence and there are a lot of people around at that time in the morning.'

'Someone he knew by sight?' It didn't bear thinking about but why else would a scared young man get into a car. John was out of his depth and he knew it. The world that Tollis knew, the clandestine world of spying on people, following them about their daily business, the sometime violence—that world was as alien to him as what he saw on the cinema screen. It was fiction come to life and he was involved in it.

'Not necessarily. A gun is pretty persuasive,' Tollis said matter-of-factly. 'Jamieson will have to know you saw Toby. You'd better phone him just to show we're willing to cooperate.'

'You won't be putting that photograph in the paper now, will you—Rees won't see it and I won't have to tell him that Toby's body's been found.'

'Rees should be told, but it's up to the doctors and there's no need to rush it.'

'And what about the person who killed Toby?' John asked quietly. 'If he finds out that the body's been found will he still look for whatever Toby had that was so important, or will he climb into a hole somewhere and hide?'

'I'm no mind-reader,' Tollis said seriously. 'If you are still worried about your own safety you should lock yourself in that flat upstairs and I'll put a man on the door. Is that what you want?'

John shook his head slowly. 'I don't want him scared off now. I want to meet him face to face, or at least be around when Jamieson takes him off to gaol.'

There was no white-hot anger in him, only something that was close to disgust. It was directed at a faceless man or men and it was becoming like a festering sore because he had no way to rid himself of it.

'I imagine that Mike feels much the same,' Tollis said.

'And there are a lot of men in Sentinel who all hope they will be the one to identify who's behind the murder. I hope you never let your anger loose, John, because you're not a violent man and I don't think you could live with it.'

'You don't know what I am—*I* don't know what I am any more. I think about these people all the time. I try to picture what they look like, where they are, and sometimes I think they're right at my elbow. I can almost feel them breathing down my neck. They're in the room when I wake up at night. And in a way it's exciting, so I'm beginning to understand why you do this job.'

'Only I don't get personally involved,' Tollis said drily. 'Phone Jamieson and tell him what you told me, then find something to keep busy with because I've got work to do.'

John spent a couple of hours going through the files Rees's secretary had left out for him and signed a pile of letters, but the silence of the empty offices finally got to him so he called it a day and decided to go and visit Rees. As he walked along the corridor he saw the decorations that the girls had hung over their desks.

The city too was strung with baubles and Princes Street was lined with Christmas trees, but it all felt out of place. Goodwill was not his prime emotion at the moment, not when he couldn't walk the streets in safety.

Rees was still hooked up to machinery and had a plastic oxygen mask over his nose and mouth. The monitor screen showed a graph of peaks and troughs that John couldn't understand, but judging by Rees's colour, he wasn't out of the wood yet.

'We had hoped to move him to the ward but the doctors want to wait a day or so yet. To be honest, he doesn't seem to have much spirit,' the nurse said. 'He's not unconscious —you can wake him.'

'Let him sleep,' John said. 'Tell him I was here when he wakes.'

When he got back to the office building Tollis told him that Arran Sinclair had returned his call. 'She'll phone back later.'

'How did she sound?'

'Uptight, disappointed you weren't here.'

'Wonder what Carrick is up to?' John murmured. 'And if he employed the Grey brothers, will he know they're dead?'

'Doubt it.' Tollis dropped a plastic coffee cup into the waste bin and then leaned forward on his elbows. 'You're convinced about him, aren't you?'

'And I don't know why. Something about the man makes the nerve endings jumpy.'

'I've followed hunches in my time,' Tollis agreed. The phone rang and he held it out to John. 'It's the hospital.'

'But I've just left there . . . Hello, this is John Leith.'

'This is Sister in CCU. Mr Kramer's condition has suddenly worsened and he's asking for you.'

'I'll be right there.' He hung up and reached for his coat. 'Rees is worse—do you want to come?'

'Of course.'

A thoughtful doctor was standing by Rees's bed with his arms folded but he waved a hand that they should go in when he saw them through the glass panelling.

'A few anxious moments but he's over it now. I'll be around if you want me.'

Rees opened his eyes and fixed them on John, then lifted a hand for him to come closer. With the other hand he pulled the mask from his face.

'Stay away from Carrick,' he said breathlessly. 'The man's insane—I should have told you all about it but I hoped nothing would come of it.'

John tried to replace the mask but Rees pushed his hand away. 'Tollis, there was no contact with Special Branch, it was all my own idea to send Toby.'

Tollis shook his head slowly from side to side but said nothing and Rees said no more either. He lapsed back into unconsciousness and John replaced the mask. The monitor continued its bleeping and they stayed for another half an hour but Rees did not open his eyes again.

'Well, Rees was up to something and the whole damn thing exploded back on him. Why?' Tollis spun the wheel of the car savagely. 'Why would a man as disciplined as Rees suddenly do something so crazy and then keep quiet about it?'

'Pride,' John said. 'Rees never had to back down and when the time came to admit he was wrong, he couldn't do it. It's like a small lie that starts a rumour that gets magnified. You pray no one will trace it back to you and as it grows and grows, you find you can't stop it anyway. I think we have to stop it—bring things to a climax in some way.'

'How do you plan to do that?'

'First, phone Arran and then maybe I'll go up there and meet Carrick in person. I've always been going to do that for days, but I've always got side-tracked. This time I won't be.'

Arran seemed glad he'd called. 'It's not that I'm on my own—although I don't have any of the women here on a Sunday—and McNeil and some of the men are around. But I thought I should let you know that Scott and some others are on their way here.'

'Thanks, that's interesting. If you like, I'll come up and keep you company.'

'Oh no, that's not necessary. Hugh is so unpredictable . . . he might not like it. I'll leave them a cold supper and stay out of their way.' She hesitated before going on: 'My mother told him you'd been up in his rooms—she lets out snippets of information as if she's trying to please him.'

'That's all right, Arran. How did he take it?'

'He was furious, of course, but his moods are like that and now I think he's forgotten all about it.'

John didn't think so. Carrick would store that up for future use.

'Don't worry about it.'

He hung up and asked Tollis if he still had men near the estate and Tollis said he had. 'But it's not very satisfactory. They're staying in the village and must stand out a mile.'

'I'm going up there. Oh, I'll be businesslike, phone Carrick in the morning, during office hours. I have the excuse of the land sale and I'll be a dumb accountant who can't see further than a page of figures.'

'Suit yourself, then. Maybe you'll be invited to stay for lunch, "and the sheep shall lie down and eat with wolves" —I think that's in the Bible somewhere.' He grinned.

'You made it up, the quotation is about liars in sheep's clothing who are really hungry wolves.'

'Same thing,' Tollis said.

CHAPTER 18

At nine he drove out to Turnhouse airport to pick up Clare and if he had any qualms about the next day, they vanished whne he saw her come into the arrivals lounge. Her dark hair swung on her shoulders and her face lit up when she saw him. It was quite something to know that that expression was solely for him. She dropped her bags and walked into his arms.

'Missed me?'

'Un-huh.' He emphasized the last word and she grinned up at him.

'I know what that means.'

He bent to kiss her smiling mouth and the other travellers parted and flowed around them, pushing them even closer together.

'Take me home,' she said.

'It might still be risky,' he warned her.

'John, I've been thinking about it for the last three days and I'm damned if I'm going to live my life to other people's rules. I want to sleep in my own bed and I want you there to keep me warm.'

So he picked up her bags and they drove to her flat in the Grange. It was a quarter of an old Victorian mansion, with three large rooms that she'd decorated in cool colours that reflected her personality. The rooms were uncluttered, the furnishings comfortable, the sort of home that welcomed and yet shut out the world. John knew it as well as his own flat, could walk into the kitchen and lay his hand on any untensil, but it remained Clare's home, not his. She'd never offered to give him a key and he'd not expected one. Strange that they'd never felt the inclination to live together and he blessed the day that he'd found a girl who was perfectly content with what they had.

'I'm going to take a bath,' she said as soon as they reached the living-room. She kicked off her shoes while he took her bags to the bedroom and then he heard the water running. Naked, she walked into the bedroom to fetch a robe and he admired the deep cleft of her spine that ended at firm buttocks, the long slender legs.

'Don't dare touch until I've washed away the smell of London,' she said over her shoulder as if guessing his thoughts. 'Go and make a pot of coffee and light the fire.'

'Spoilsport,' he sighed.

She was pink and glowing when she joined him. Her hair was damp but tied back from her face, and she looked about seventeen, but the expression in her eyes was far from immature. 'Don't really want the coffee,' she said softly and he saw her nipples showing hard against the thin fabric of the robe. So they lay in front of the fire in soft lamplight with the homely smell of coffee filling the room, and her body, perfumed from her bath, under him. The rhythms were gentle and infinitely loving, sweeter because they'd been apart.

'Shower,' he said and then both stood under the jets, soaping each other's bodies until desire overtook them again. The long night became a honeymoon until they fell asleep in each other's arms early in the morning. At eight John slipped out of the bed and dressed. He was in Rees's office just before nine to phone the Sinclair estate to let them know he was coming, and by ten he was half way up the motorway to Perth. His body was relaxed despite the lack of sleep.

He had brought all the survey reports on the land that was to be sold, along with notes on the suggested publicity and he had gone over it until he was word perfect.

'Take someone with you,' Tollis had urged. 'Someone

from the valuation department, just to give it authenticity.'
But John had refused.

'Well, don't try to be clever and you've no legitimate
interest in Scott, remember.'

'I've no plans. I'm playing it by ear and I won't take
chances with two women there.'

Jamieson had phoned too and he'd been abrupt. 'I'm
against you going up there,' he said. 'It's only a matter of
time before we have the lot of them in.'

'But you can't act yet, can you?'

'If Rees Kramer could make a statement we'd make our
move, but at the moment we've nothing to hold them on,'
Jamieson agreed. 'You could scare them off.'

'Are you ordering me not to go?'

'I can't do that, Mr Leith. Just offer advice.'

'Then I'll promise to be careful but if I can stir things
up, I will.'

He'd hung up and now he didn't feel in the least nervous,
just keyed up. His mind was sharp and even his vision
seemed crystal clear, but he knew he had a pose to main-
tain. He was a man struggling to carry on his uncle's business, a man bewildered by recent events that he couldn't
begin to understand. No suspicion of Carrick or Scott must
intrude in his manner. He was playing dumb, dumb, dumb.

He drove around the main house and pulled up in the
open-sided quadrangle and as usual the ever watchful
McNeil was there as he got out of the car. He was delighted
to see John.

'Man, I'm glad that Miss Arran will have company in
the house—that bastard won't have me in.'

'Is he in?'

'No. He took the horse out, no doubt he's flogging the
poor beast. The rest are inside, though—they've no
stomach for good clean air and the house stinks of their
cigars and cigarettes.'

'How many?'

'Three men and one woman—would you credit him bringing her here?' McNeil shook his head as they stepped inside the porch but just then the clatter of hooves made them swing around to see Carrick slide down from the back of his steaming horse.

'What did I say? Just look at that animal—I'll away and see to it.' And McNeil hurried off without introducing the two men.

Carrick was wearing the full riding gear right down to polished boots and he swung his crop against them as he marched towards John. His stride was jerky, as if the ride had done nothing to rid him of surplus energy, but he slowed when he raised his head and spotted John waiting for him.

'Well?'

'I'm from Kramer's, about the land sale,' John said and Carrick brushed past him with a curt 'You'd better come in, then.'

He walked quickly along the corridor that John had already travelled on his last visit, the sound of his boots warning those ahead in the living quarters that he was coming. The door at the end of the passage opened and John saw it was the sitting-room where he'd had tea with Lorna and Arran, but now there were three men and a woman in it. They looked curiously at John but the woman —Jane Freeman—spoke to Carrick.

'How was the ride, then?'

'Bloody animal hasn't been properly exercised,' he grumbled, dropping into a chair.

The man sitting in shadow at the far wall spoke up. He was the one who had not taken his eyes from John since he entered the room. 'Who's your guest, Hugh?' he asked quietly and it was a rebuke to Carrick's bad manners. That

was how it was taken anyway, because everyone else looked
to Carrick nervously, but he didn't seem put out.

'From Kramer's.'

The other man nodded and waited for more. The girl in
a body-hugging black pant suit had been curled up in her
chair, but now she moved restlessly, as if somehow the
rebuke affected all in the room. And John could understand
that, because the man—Scott, he presumed—dominated
the room with his presence. Carrick must be super-
insensitive, he thought, not to feel the tension in the air.

He decided to speak up for himself, mindful of the rôle
he had chosen to play. 'Rees Kramer has had a heart attack
and I'm trying to deal with outstanding business.' He
shrugged apologetically. 'I'm an accountant, used to dealing with figures, not up on property, I'm afraid, but I'm
here to finalize some details. Is there anywhere we can
talk?' he asked Carrick directly.

'You forgot to mention your name,' Scott said with
another gentle nudge at protocol. He was an oily character,
John decided; the sort of man who squirmed his way into
a gathering, played the quiet observer while all the time
picking up tips and information. On his own ground he
would be ruthless. That much came across quite clearly
and no doubt there was a lot more below the surface.

'John Leith; Rees Kramer is my uncle.'

Carrick's head jerked around at that and for the first time
he looked John fully in the face. His eyes travelled over the
stitch line, lingered on the bruises and then smiled.

'Had an accident, Mr Leith?'

The girl sniggered but was silenced by a look from Scott.

'We don't need to discuss the land—I've already disposed of it,' Carrick snapped and he looked pleased at
John's obvious surprise. 'No fat commission for Kramer's
after all.'

Scott's quiet interruption fell into the silence like a balm.

'Now, Hugh, don't be rude when Mr Leith's come so far. He deserves an explanation at the very least. Shouldn't you ask him to stay for lunch?' He stood up and came towards John, who now saw that he was less than six feet tall but his age was hard to determine because his dark hair was receding, but around fifty, he thought. His suit was expensively cut but there was none of the ostentation that Carrick seemed to like. He could pass through a crowd unnoticed; he could be anyone's nice father, older caring brother, except perhaps for the eyes which were grey and cold and that hard-to-disguise menacing chill that was like an aura around him. John was quite certain now that Scott was dangerous, was probably the faceless man he'd been trying so hard to meet face to face.

'You see, Mr Leith, the business of the land is not quite settled. There is a strip that runs along the river that is essential for the development, but Arran can't be persuaded to part with it. Perhaps with you here she might discuss it. It would be very much to her advantage to at least listen to the arguments, but up to now the young lady shows no interest.'

Carrick suddenly lost his temper and came out of his seat. 'I told you I'd get her to sign the bloody papers. We don't need outsiders poking their noses in. He's —' and here Carrick pointed a stabbing finger in John's direction —'he's already been here, sniffing into things that don't concern him.' He came closer, anger distorting his features so that instead of being a handsome man, he was now ugly, with his face suffused with blood, eyes popping, lips drawn back in a snarl that made John think 'mad dog'. He was frightening in his anger, but Scott stood almost lazily in front of him until Carrick expelled a long, whisky-laden breath.

'Hugh,' Scott said with a gentle reproof, 'why don't you

go and get changed for lunch—Jane, you go with him—
while Mr Leith and I have a talk.'

'I agree with him,' John said mildly. 'I can't advise Miss
Sinclair. Her lawyer should be here to do that.'

Carrick passed both of them without a glance and let the
door slam behind him. The girl slid from her seat with a
shrug and followed sulkily. The other two men, who so far
had not said a word, sat like statues, and it was easy to
forget that they were present. Scott repeated his invitation.

'Stay as an observer, then. Arran will at least join us for
lunch if you are here.'

And John accepted, but not for any of the reasons that
would have pleased Scott. He had to try to find out more,
and with Carrick so volatile he might just give something
away. And he wanted to act as a buffer for Arran.

'That's fine,' Scott said, seeming more pleased than he
should have been, which made John feel as if a gate had
swung shut behind him. He had walked into this with his
eyes open and now it was up to him to act out the charade.

CHAPTER 19

Scott and his silent companions went up to their rooms to pack because they were leaving after lunch and John went outside for fresh air and in the hope of a chat with McNeil. There was no sign of Arran and he wasn't sure if she knew he was there.

McNeil was in one of the stables, watching Carrick's horse get a final rub down. 'Aye, he's fine now.' He was still angry with Carrick's treatment, though. 'Horses are special creatures and I can't abide a man who abuses them. I'll be glad when he's away out of here.'

'The others are leaving after lunch but I don't know if he's going with them,' John said.

McNeil nodded. 'He has that boat of his in Edinburgh and I did hear him say he might go out in her. Och, let's take a bit of a stroll, Mr Leith. I like to see how things are going at this time of the day.'

John had the feeling that McNeil had other things on his mind, and he was right.

'The fact is that I'm near seventy-five and I can't see what's around the corner for Miss Arran. Can she make a go of it, do you think? All this talk of developing that land across the river . . . What happens to the visitors we get? Who'll come here if they can get all the trappings like golf and swimming across there?'

'Is that the plan?'

'Oh aye. Luxury bungalows with everything they'll need and a leisure place where you can get a sauna or the ladies can get a facial . . . We dinna even have central heating!' He stopped, hands deep in the pockets of his cords, face grim. 'There's no competing with the likes of that, I'm thinking.'

'Not everyone wants that kind of luxury,' John said, but he didn't sound encouraging and McNeil understood.

'No, maybe not, but it wouldn't take much to finish us off. I never thought I'd see the day when Graham Sinclair's place would go bust.' They walked back towards the house, John for the lunch to which McNeil was not invited, and they parted at the stables.

Arran had not changed her normal eating arrangements and the lunch was served at the long table in the kitchen. She had even kept on her working clothes and although she had a smile of welcome for John, she was formal with the others.

John sat next to her at the table, the others were already seated but Carrick was last to arrive and he sat next to Jane Freeman at the far end from John.

Scott wasted no time and explained they were leaving right after the meal. 'But I'd like you to give some last thoughts to that stretch of land.' Arran was already stubbornly shaking her head but Scott ignored that and went right on.

He had little charm and it seemed to be an effort for him to be pleasantly persuasive. There was an implied threat that he wasn't going to take no for an answer and although the persuasive tone was soft, his hooded eyes were remorseless. He was not used to being refused what he had set his mind on acquiring.

'What value would you place on that land, Mr Leith?'

'I think it depends on how much you want it. That's how property prices are usually settled, according to my uncle.' He spoke mildly, aware of the flash of anger in Scott's eyes, but Scott was not to be put off.

'Then we can negotiate, with Mr Leith as referee—if that's the correct word?'

John carefully sliced up his chicken, trying to hide his own anger and preserve his rôle of ignorant deputy for Rees.

'I don't think that works unless both parties are willing.'

Around the table heads were lowered over food, as if everyone not taking part was trying hard not to get involved, with the exception of Hugh Carrick who was beginning to steam again. Even Scott was losing patience. Had he really thought that Arran would crumble just because he expected it of her? No doubt he thought that everyone had a price and had never met anyone who didn't think money was everything. After all, how could he believe that anyone would want to hang on to an estate that was run down and still going downhill? John could just imagine the conversation between him and Carrick before coming to Scotland. '*Of course she'll take the cash. You've not handled her properly—she's just a woman, after all.*' But the woman had backbone and a home that she loved beyond any money, and Scott was just beginning to find that out. How would he take the refusal? John was poised for a violent outburst, but Arran delayed it somewhat.

'Does this mean that you bought my land from Hugh?' she asked.

Scott hesitated, then plunged into an explanation of sorts. 'I'm part of a company that will develop it. And you're asking us to draw a line when the river is a more natural boundary.'

'The river is part of our business plan too,' she pointed out. 'But that isn't the real reason you want it, is it? You want to build an airstrip there—it's common knowledge here. You've applied for planning permission and you can't keep that sort of thing secret. Planes flying over my land, disturbing the deer and my guests—it's not on. The answer is no, I won't sell that land.' And there was a finality in her tone that Scott couldn't miss. He looked stunned when she revealed that she knew his plans. It was a real put-down to his arguments and for a moment he looked lost for words, but Carrick's chair scraped back and he came to his feet.

'I warned you,' he raged, lifting the heavy table as he rose, so that the water glasses tilted and spilled their contents. 'Too many outsiders knowing what we were going to do . . . Kramer interfering . . .' He moved towards Arran and although Scott tried to grab his arm as he passed, he shrugged him off. He was on the wrong side of the table for John to intervene, so along with everyone else he rose to try to grab him before he reached Arran. It happened swiftly after that, with Carrick pulling Arran from her seat and along with him towards the door.

'You fool, you'll spoil everything,' Scott called after him, but Carrick appeared to be deaf and although Arran struggled she made no impression on him either.

Scott waved to his two accomplices, who moved like professionals now, but Carrick had slipped the bolt on the door to the porch and precious seconds were lost as the men had to kick it free of its screws. Carrick paused at the door to one of the stables.

'I'll show you what people understand and it's not sweet talk,' he shouted. Then he pulled Arran inside. Around the work area, men had frozen into a tableau of statues, but now they began to move, slowly at first and than at a run. Scott's men were already near the stable when a shot rang out and that halted everyone. The scream that followed could have been human or animal and John felt a chill pass through his body. With the rest he moved forward and stopped again when Carrick appeared with a rifle in his hand. He's mad, he was thinking, when Carrick reloaded and pointed the rifle straight at John's body.

'And you, you pen-pusher, always it comes down to you.' He no longer had a dazed look but was coldly menacing and his intent was clear. John was preparing himself to feel a bullet smashing into his body, saw Carrick's finger begin to tighten on the trigger, when Arran threw herself at her stepfather. As they struggled the gun went off harmlessly into the air, and then Scott's man had him. The rifle was wrenched from his hands, the stock was swung to connect with the point of his jaw, and Carrick collapsed, loose-limbed, on to the stable floor.

McNeil was first to reach Arran but she pointed behind her and McNeil went to the horse that was stretched out on the straw.

'I'll need that,' he said, pointing to the gun. 'He's shot her horse and he couldn't even make a proper job of that.'

Arran was weeping and as another shot rang out she turned and leaned against the rough harling of the building. John, still shocked at the turn of events, went to ease her away and lead her back to the house. He left Scott standing alongside the angry estate workers. Jane Freeman was shivering and looking scared but no one was paying her any attention. He got the woman who worked in the kitchen to stay with Arran and then went back to see that Scott and his men left.

'My business here is not finished by any means,' Scott told him before getting into his car. 'We'll take Carrick with us for Miss Sinclair's sake, but the man needs treatment. I presume there's no need for the police to be called in?'

'That's not up to me,' John told him. 'And if you think you have any further business here, just look around you. This is a community that sticks together and you haven't a hope of getting local support.'

Scott was not ruffled and he even smiled slightly. 'I wondered how long you could keep it up. A man with as many lives as you have is not to be underestimated. That was Hugh's first mistake. But now I'm taking over and I don't lose—ever. We don't need local support, Mr Leith, just paper money—that can buy anything in this world.'

John prevented him from closing the door. 'Why?' he said. 'What was it all about?'

Scott knew exactly what he meant. 'You had something

I wanted, but Carrick couldn't handle it. He's bungled everything from the beginning.'

'I don't know what that something is,' John said.

'Obviously,' Scott said, stony-faced. 'Let's hope it's gone forever, shall we? If it turns up you'll know, and then you can bring it to me. That way you'll save yourself any further . . . grief.'

'Go to hell,' John said succinctly.

Carrick was coming around. 'I'm not finished with you, you bastard,' he muttered, shaking off restraining hands. 'Just wait.'

Scott sighed. 'I should be careful if I were you. He's a fool and he's no longer of any use to me—he'll blame you for that as well, I expect.'

John phoned Tollis as soon as he could. 'I think your men would be of more use up here at the house. Arran needs to feel that Carrick can't come back.'

'I'll arrange it. Get back as soon as you can. Jamieson is coming around later and I'd like him to hear all this.'

John hung up. There wasn't anything he could do to console Arran, so he waited until Tollis's men arrived and then left. He had a lot to think about as he drove back to Edinburgh, especially the casual coldness in Scott's eyes.

CHAPTER 20

'Well, that's all very interesting but we've no proof of any kind,' Jamieson said. 'But your uncle seems to know more than he's told you so far—what's his condition, is he likely to be able to make a statement?'

'I don't know.' Rees, the man he would have backed to be honest through and through, the man of integrity, had somehow been involved with Carrick and Scott.

'And we still don't know what they've been looking for all this time.' Jamieson looked frustrated. 'But we *do* know that the bullet removed from Toby Cairns's skull did not come from the gun that the Greys had. The one that killed your man was a .22 and we found the cartridge case near the body. From the powder burns we know the gun was held not more than two feet from him—if he was conscious he knew what was about to happen. It was a cold-blooded killing. The PM report is quite detailed and we know he was killed on the day that Mr Leith's office was broken into, so that fits.'

'How can you be certain?'

'Don't ask,' Tollis warned, but Jamieson told them a little anyway.

'It has to do with the life cycle of the maggots in the body, Mr Leith, and other things—I don't think you really want to go into that. I'll arrange for a search of the estate, I think, to see if Carrick has hand guns as well as rifles. And he didn't go to Glasgow with the rest, by the way, he's still here in Edinburgh, staying with Jane Freeman. We're keeping an eye on them.'

'Why can't you arrest him?' Tollis asked. 'He did kill that horse and he threatened to kill John.'

'Both he and Scott will be questioned about their alibis for the Cairns killing, but what happened up at the estate is . . . well, to be honest I'd rather be patient and get him for the lot.'

'The next time,' John said drily. 'Only that might mean he's killed me.'

'We're watching him,' Jamieson repeated. 'Now let's review the probable sequence of events from the beginning. Rees Kramer sent Toby Cairns to Albert Gumley's—your father-in-law's house—for reasons we don't yet understand. Step one—I'll see Gumley again. Cairns found out something and passed the information to you, Mr Leith, but we don't know what form that took and it is presumably now lost. That something was important to Tony Scott, and Carrick was given the job of recovering it, hence all your mishaps. Scott had no record of convictions, by the way, but he's known as being involved in gambling clubs where drugs are passed and recently he was suspected of murdering a young woman, but he had a very good alibi. The police in the west would dearly like to get evidence to convict him. In the meantime, he has acquired land that Carrick was selling. Did Carrick look like a man who had just received a large payment for land?'

'No. I did wonder if Carrick needed the money to pay off debts and maybe Scott held the markers.'

'That sounds likely, which would leave Carrick a sour and bitter man after all the trouble he's gone to.' Jamieson seemed pleased with the résumé. 'You see how all the bits of the jigsaw are coming together?'

'But all the important bits are missing,' Tollis said gloomily.

'Patience. One more small thing could make it all complete and I always think it's vital to know the characters and to work out their motives. Then you know how they

will react when something else develops. What feelings did
you have about Scott?' he asked John.

'That he doesn't like being crossed. He said himself that
he wasn't giving up on that land.'

Jamieson had both hands joined as in prayer, tapping
his fingers against the sides of his nose. 'That airstrip. He
must have been furious that word had got out about that.
What do you think of a man suspected of handling drugs
who acquires a small airstrip in a quiet area like that? Then
he's frustrated because he can't get all the land he needs to
make it happen. He's already written off a lot of cash and
you'll never convince me that he's desperate to get into the
time-share business. He has far more at stake.'

'It doesn't fit Scott's image,' Tollis said, leaning forward.
'The profits are not certain.'

Jamieson seemed satisfied that they'd talked it all out.
'Now we do as much digging as we can, and we wait,' he
said, getting to his feet. 'I'll keep in touch.'

And after he'd gone, Tollis got up and stretched. 'Let's
go visit Rees,' he growled. 'I want to do my own chewing
at the bone. Jamieson sees everything from a policeman's
angle, far too logical for me.'

They walked on pavements greasy with the last of the
slush mixed with the city's grime, shoulders hunched into
a chill wind that felt as if it was coming across the North
Sea from Siberia. The city was quiet, with few people
around, and even the rather grand, if sooty, buildings of
the Infirmary were curiously deserted.

'Gwen and Janet have been landed with all the visiting
hours,' John said. 'Rees doesn't seem to have many friends.'

'Never had time to make any,' Tollis said, but both knew
that there were other reasons. Rees didn't need anything
apart from his work, and friends made demands. Friends
expected a certain amount of closeness, openness, and Rees
was not a sociable man.

They passed a long line of silent ambulances outside the accident unit where John had been a casualty on the day the intruder had struck him down—it seemed an age ago. John paused outside the glass doors that led to the corridor of wards.

'How do we handle this if Rees is up to talking?'

'I think he'll tell it all now. There won't be any question of dragging it out of him.'

In the event they were not allowed to see Rees. 'He's being prepared for an angiogram,' a nurse explained. 'The consultant wants to see what's going on, so an injection of dye will show up how the blood vessels are behaving.'

'Can he stand up to that?'

'It can be risky, but it's necessary.'

'Poor Rees, he'll hate being mucked about,' Tollis said as they walked back to the High Street. 'Why did he keep all this to himself . . . it's bugging me. And he lied. He said at first that it was a Special Branch job.'

'I've just remembered something he said that first night he was admitted to hospital. He said sorry, that it was all meant for the best. I thought he was sorry to be a nuisance —which would be just like him, to apologize for having a heart attack, but it wasn't that at all. He was trying to explain.' John sighed. 'I'm sorry for him. He started all this and I think it's killing him. I'll go back to Gumley's tomorrow—he knows much more than he's telling us and Jamieson won't get it out of him. Gumley's dying and he's not afraid of the police.'

Tollis wanted to go for a drink but John didn't feel that they would achieve anything more by sitting speculating. 'I think I'll drive up to Clare's and take her out for supper.'

'At least there's no more danger from Carrick and Co. Jamieson will have them all under surveillance,' Tollis said.

So why, John wondered, did he still feel like glancing over his shoulder?

Grange Park Road, where Clare had her flat, was a badly lit road and always clogged with residents' cars. Tonight was no exception and he had nearly twenty yards to walk back after he'd found a parking space. With the square shapes of the houses on his right almost hidden behind well-established shrubberies and trees, the street was an ideal place for an ambush, but the only living creature he saw was a cat.

He nearly fell over it in the gloom and it spat at him before snaking into a garden. The silence was welcome and the prospect of a quiet evening with Clare made him quicken his pace. He imagined her out of her office clothes, relaxing to music and planning an easy supper she could eat in front of the fire.

It was as far removed from Carrick and the troubles of the estate that he could hope to get, so when he put his finger on the bell he was already feeling the tension seep out of him.

'Come in. I was hoping you'd turn up—it saved me making a phone call,' said Hugh Carrick. The light was behind him but it gave the gun in his hand a dull menacing gleam. 'Miss Aitken will be relieved too, I think.'

CHAPTER 21

'What have you done to her?' John pushed past Carrick who was lit up like a child before a birthday party. His eyes had a manic gleam and his face shone with a film of sweat. John ignored the gun, stepped into the square hallway and then moved towards the sitting-room, the source of the light.

Clare was sitting in a chair by the fire, apparently unhurt but frozen with terror. How long had she been alone with Carrick and that gun, probably listening to his ravings? Her lips had been compressed but when she saw him it was as if her control almost snapped and tears filled her eyes. Somehow she managed to stop them overflowing and her chin came up in a defiant gesture that John recognized. It was like a two-fingered sign to Carrick, but it also told John that she still had fight in her. He crossed the room and took her in his arms and he could feel her body trembling.

'He's waiting for a phone call,' she whispered with her face turned up to his.

'That's right,' Carrick said from close behind and John turned to face him, putting his body in front of Clare. The gun was held steadily and it was hard to take his eyes from it but he had to, to try to read Carrick's intentions. The man was dishevelled, his clothes strained as if he'd slid on wet grass. Green streaks soiled the arms and front of his polo-necked sweater and there were other stains that looked like soot. He held Carrick's gaze, took in the vivid blue swelling on the point of his chin where the rifle butt had struck him, the feverish look in his eyes.

'A phone call and then I'll be able to leave,' Carrick breathed. He smiled, teeth white against the tan and the dirt and John was reminded of the nursery rhyme, the wolf huffing and puffing to bring the house down.

'Why here? Why come here for a phone call?' he asked, but he already knew the answer. He kept one hand behind him, holding Clare in his shadow and he was surprised that his voice sounded so calm when his heartbeat was tripping along like a piston out of control.

Carrick grinned again, his mouth distorted by the swelling beneath it. 'Because you care about her and what happens to her,' he said sortly. Hate flared in his eyes, like a sudden gleam from a beacon on a foggy night. 'I could have been long gone but first I had to settle with you. You've taken it all from me and now I'll take everything you love. All of it.' The voice was quiet, every word loaded with menace, and John knew that Carrick intended to kill them both. Curiously, it was a relief to face his enemy instead of constantly wondering who he was. Behind him he heard Clare's indrawn breath but she didn't move. Perhaps Carrick would expect him to beg for her life.

'Sit over there, away from her,' Carrick ordered with a sweep of the gun. John didn't move.

'Do it or I'll kill her,' Carrick said and there was no emotion in the tone at all. It didn't matter to him if John obeyed or not; John moved slowly to the other side of the fire and sat down. The room was very warm. The gas fire was on full and yet the sweat that trickled down between his shoulder-blades was cold.

'Now we just have to wait,' Carrick said pleasantly, as if they were waiting for tea to be served. John could now see the whole of the man and he saw that his cords too were filthy, as if he'd crawled through a sewer. The hand holding the gun was dirty, the knuckles grazed, and Carrick, as if reading his thoughts, was nodding smugly.

'They were watching the flat but they let Jane out to buy food. I went over the roof. It's flat at the back and further

along there was scaffolding. All over Edinburgh they're
tarting up the old buildings and no one notices the scaffolding any more. It was easy to come down in the alley and I
just walked away. They'll be wondering why Jane's taking
so long to buy fish suppers, or maybe they've already discovered that we're both gone.' He laughed with delight and
it sounded so natural that it was hard to believe that in a
few moments he might point the gun at them and kill them
both. The man was dangerous, with swings of mood that
were unpredictable, and John wondered how to handle him.

'Tollis knows I'm here so this is the first place they'll
check,' he said calmly.

'That's even better, adds the spice, don't you think?' The
laugh was out of control this time and ended on a high
note. The gun hand wavered and John calculated how
many seconds it would take for him to dive at the man, but
Carrick's finger was tight on the trigger. John could see the
white skin around the joint of the finger and he knew that
Carrick was longing to put a bullet in him but for some
reason he was controlling the urge. For how long? Until the
phone rang?

'I could do with a Scotch,' he said, and to his surprise
Carrick agreed. In fact, the instant he mentioned it he saw
Carrick's tongue come out to lick his dry lips. 'Got any,
Clare?'

He spoke directly to her, trying to reassure her that everything would be all right.

She was pale, with her hands clasped tightly in the lap
of her jeans, but she was in control again and he could
see she had read his message by the small tight smile she
managed. But Carrick wasn't going to let her move around.

'You get it,' he snapped. 'Try anything and I'll shoot
her.'

John tried for some more leeway. 'First I want to take
this off,' he said, struggling out of his anorak. Carefully he

folded it and laid it on the arm of the chair—that would give him more freedom of movement should he get the chance. Then he got up and moved to the drinks tray and set out three glasses, poured the Scotch without spilling a drop. He took one for himself and one for Clare. Carrick stood well back, alert, until he was seated. It was like a badly directed play, he thought, with the actors not sure of their places. No chance to throw the liquid in Carrick's face anyway. Carrick tossed his back quickly and at that moment the phone rang.

They all jumped and Carrick almost dropped the receiver in his rush to pick it up. 'Where the hell have you been?' he screamed. 'Yes, yes,' impatiently, and John guessed that Jane Freeman was on the other end. 'Yes!' Carrick said again and the change in him was dramatic. He was triumphant, bursting with it so that his lips were slack with relief.

He slammed the phone down and spun around. 'Now, John Leith,' and his gun hand came up, but suddenly he turned, aimed at Clare and fired.

It was so sudden. No last-minute warning threats, not a hint of what was to come, but Clare turned slightly at the last moment, her face frozen in an expression of horror.

As if in slow motion John rose, saw the blood run through her fingers on her chest. 'You bastard!' he shouted. Clare's eyes were closed and she slumped in her seat, the bloodstain spread rapidly, and Carrick watched with lips apart and sheer satisfaction in his eyes. The man was gloating, and something snapped in John's brain. He lunged, fingers reaching for Carrick's throat.

Carrick was faster and he moved back. 'She's still alive,' he shouted, and it was a warning that somehow penetrated the red-hot rage. Carrick had swung the gun back on Clare and John had to pull himself up. He crouched, arms still spread wide, his breath coming in anguished sobs of rage.

Carrick nodded, pleased that he still had the upper hand and that his enemy was suffering sufficiently.

'I'm a good shot, Leith. I can kill her easily from here but she can live if you do exactly as I say.'

'I'm not helping you get away,' John vowed.

'No. Then I'll cut off the phone before I shoot you in the stomach and you'll die slowly, watching your lady friend bleed to death. That tickle your fancy? It's time I was on my way and you're coming with me. Make your choice.'

'An ambulance,' John said, making a move towards the phone, but Carrick didn't like that and the gun came up in line with his middle.

'She must get to hospital,' John said hoarsely and he walked past Carrick and picked up the phone, expecting to feel the slam of a bullet in his back. He dialled the first 9 before Carrick intervened again.

'We have your son,' he said softly. 'That phone call was to say that Jane had picked him up.'

John let the phone fall.

'I don't believe you. Gwen would never let a stranger take him away from Elmwood.'

'She wasn't there—it was the housekeeper. Jane pretended she was my stepdaughter, the nice Arran Sinclair who was a friend of the boy's father. The message was that you wanted him here in town and she even combed his hair first to make him presentable for his dear daddy.'

John felt the skin on his face contract because he knew it was probably true. Janet had heard of Arran but she'd never met her. Carrick had meant it when he threatened to take away all he loved. All. That meant Clare and David. And he was keeping John alive so that he could witness both killings. It was the way of the sadist.

'What a way to get your kicks,' he said evenly. 'When I pick up the phone to call for an ambulance, you can shoot me in the back if you like but that will spoil the fun, won't it? I won't be around to beg for my son's life.' He saw the indecision on Carrick's face before he turned to pick up the phone again, and then he dialled 999.

'Urgently, please, it's a bullet wound,' he told the operator. Then he gave the address, speaking distinctly.

'And now,' he told Carrick, 'I'm going to get the duvet from the bed to cover her.'

His legs felt stiff as he walked to and from the bedroom but Carrick didn't move as he tucked it around her gently. Her skin was cold and her breathing was shallow but the wound was above her heart. She's alive, he told himself, and she'll be all right. He wanted to take her in his arms and hold her until the ambulance came, but even if Carrick allowed it he knew he daren't move her. He brushed her dark glossy hair back from her face and bent to kiss her cold forehead and that was when Carrick snapped.

'Enough. Move,' he said tersely, jerking the gun towards the door. They went out into the night, with John making sure that both doors were left open so that nothing would delay the ambulance men from reaching Clare. Again there was the twenty-yard walk to his car, and no residents to witness them pulling away from the kerb. How long, he wondered, before a report reached Jamieson?

A bullet wound automatically involved the police but would those called to Clare's home connect up with those searching for Carrick and Jane Freeman? Only Jamieson would spot the significance and then the major hunt would begin, but by then it might be far too late.

'I take it we're heading for Granton?' he said as they approached the junction at the end of the street and he felt Carrick stiffen beside him—good, he enjoyed delivering that news. 'McNeil told me you had *Sea Princess* ready for a trip.'

'Who else knows?'

John shrugged carelessly. 'No idea who else he told, but

it's common knowledge that you own a yacht and someone will put two and two together.' It was an effort to give Carrick a stiff humourless grin but he managed it. 'Adds to the suspense, doesn't it? Will we find a reception committee on the quay?'

He could smell the man's sweat, fetid, sour. Carrick, who was fastidious about himself and his appearance, would hate that and the state of his clothes. Well, anything, however small, that threw the man off balance was a point in John's favour.

'Take Broughton Street, then through Goldenacre,' Carrick said as they came off North Bridge. 'Don't do anything to attract attention.' So John kept to a steady thirty and tried to think of other things to needle him.

Carrick was sitting side on, without his seat-belt, and every so often he glanced out of the back window to see if they were being followed. John considered stamping on the accelerator and then braking hard in the hope that Carrick would go through the windscreen, or perhaps slamming into a parked car, but neither offered a certain solution when there was a gun pointing at him. And the car, kept in tip-top condition by the Kramer team, was not likely to break down or suffer a puncture. Time was running out as his mind flitted through all the possibilities but at the back of his mind was the image of David on board the yacht, frightened.

'You haven't a hope, you know. They'll notify the coast-guard and then every ship will be asked to look out for you.'

'The sea's a big place and I'll take my chances.' Carrick ground out the words and John knew the man wasn't going to back down now, even from murder.

They were looking down on the River Forth now and could clearly see the lights of the Fife coastline on the opposite shore, and he knew that from now on he would just have to grab whatever presented itself.

'Stop here for a bit,' Carrick said. They were still above the harbour and Carrick had obviously been worried by John's hint that they might face a reception committee. Carrick leaned forward to check, but there were no police vehicles, no vehicles at all near the quay.

He made John stop when short of the quay and they got out to walk the rest. The sea slapping against hulls was the only sound apart from their footsteps and when the moon disappeared behind a cloud John slowed, hoping to get a chance to tackle Carrick, but the man kept his distance. It was very dark, apart from the distant reflections of street lights on the water and the occasional glimpse of the moon. The quay was paved with uneven stones but Carrick was sure-footed and never once stumbled.

Then they were looking down on *Sea Princess* and John saw that she was a Westerly 27, easy for Carrick to manage single-handed, so it didn't matter if Jane Freeman was a novice. He had hoped that the yacht would be at a free-swinging mooring, which would have meant rowing out to her, but instead she was at the side of the quay, all of eighteen feet below them, rolling on the choppy waves.

'You first,' Carrick said, and John swing himself on to the vertical ladder. The rungs were rusted and icy in his hands and the freezing wind tore through his clothes. Lower down there was seaweed clinging to the metal and just as he jumped the last few feet the wet weed made him slip and he almost went into the water. Instead, he fell over the guard rail clumsily and rolled on the foredeck. Carrick sniggered as he began his own descent.

It was a very long time since John had been on board any sort of boat and all the old fears he'd felt as a child were very easy to remember now.

However, other memories came back too, of the things that were kept on deck which could be handy as weapons. The darkness was his ally and as he lay on his side, he scrabbled around, feeling for anything useful, like the thick knotted ball on the end of a heaving line known as a monkey's fist that his father showed him how to make, but not likely to be one of Carrick's talents—oh, for a rocket pistol, he sighed, but that would be secured. His fingers closed on cold metal. The bilge pump handle, nearly eighteen inches long and about two inches thick had been left there carelessly and he grasped it firmly, measured the weight of it, balanced it and knew it was his last chance. Carrick was on deck now.

'Get up,' he said shortly, easily getting his sea legs and not at all put out by the roll of his boat. John rose, with the metal bar behind him and in the darkness Carrick didn't notice anything amiss.

'I've sprained my ankle,' John said. To prove it, he put his foot down and then collapsed again. His heart was thudding as he prayed for Carrick to come closer, but Carrick was suspicious. 'Look, for Christ's sake, I'm hardly likely to jump into the sea or back up there, am I?' John snapped, rubbing his ankle.

To his relief Carrick came forward, the gun half raised. The man was in his element, feeling safe. There had been no police cars on the quay, no suggestion of a chase at all. What indeed could John Leith do to escape now?

When he was close enough John swung the pump handle upwards in a vicious swing that caught Carrick's gun hand. He heard a bone snap and Carrick screamed in pain; the gun sailed out over the side to land in the sea with a satisfying plop. 'Now,' John said, jumping to his feet. 'Where's my son?' But there were other weapons on the yacht and Carrick knew exactly where they were. He backed off and reached out with his good left hand and came up with a boat-hook.

His face was grimacing with pain as he crouched, feet wide spread, and stabbed John viciously in the ribs. Carrick had two advantages; the longer weapon, and he knew the confined space of his own boat. John had to cling to the stays to keep his balance as the boat rolled and there just wasn't enough room to avoid Carrick's lunges. He tried to knock the boat-hook aside but when Carrick got up on the coach roof he had no chance to stay out of his reach. Carrick put his injured right arm around the mast and John suffered blows as Carrick stabbed with the boat-hook or swung it. And all the time, Carrick spat out curses. His mouth drooled with them as he savoured his moment of revenge.

'First you, then your brat.' He described exactly how David would meet his end. 'I'll dangle him over the side a bit—' lunge and crack as he hit John's elbow and sent pain shooting down to his fingers. 'Then I'll duck him now and then just to prolong things. The water's cold, deadly cold —' another stabbing thrust caught John's shoulder and sent him spinning but his outflung arm caught a stay and saved him from going over the side. Carrick was gasping for breath, but still he taunted, and so far John had not got close enough to do any more damage. It would have been all over by now if Carrick's right hand had not been broken.

Then Carrick paused and John found himself trapped with no chance of ducking what was to be the final lunge. Both were sucking in great gulps of air, but Carrick showed no signs of weakening and John knew it had to be now or never. While Carrick gloated prematurely, his chest heaving for air, John drew back his arm and threw the heavy metal bar like a javelin. Carrick had no chance to avoid it and it took him in the centre of his forehead with a dull sickening thud. For a few seconds he stood on the coach roof, swaying, unconscious, but with eyes still wide open as if shocked that he was the loser. Then *Sea Princess* rolled and sent her master over the side into the icy water. He landed flat in an untidy splash but he had disappeared before John dragged himself to look over at the oily surface.

There was no body to be seen and no change in the pattern of the waves. Hugh Carrick had drifted away in the darkness or sunk below the surface and John didn't give a damn. He heaved himself up as Jane Freeman spoke from behind him.

'Where's Hugh?'

She must have been watching them, must have heard Carrick fall over the side. Was she hoping he'd fish the bastard out?

'Half way to hell,' he said brusquely as he pushed by her. David was asleep in the small fo'c's'le, and even when John lifted him he didn't waken. 'David? Did you give him anything?' he demanded, but Jane Freeman was curled up on a bunk in the outer compartment and she refused to look at him.

'Hugh said to give him some pills but I only gave him one,' she muttered.

The quay was alight with blue police lamps when he came on deck with David in his arms.

'We were going sailing, Dad,' David suddenly murmured.

'Some other time, son. It's a bit rough tonight,' John told him, holding him tightly against his bruised ribs. One day soon he would tell David some of it, but for now he was just glad that his son had no idea of the danger he'd been in. Other arms lifted David to the quay and then leaned down to help John back up the ladder.

Only then did he feel his bruises, and his exhaustion was such that he could barely lift his legs. His first question was for Clare, but no one knew if she was still alive.

CHAPTER 22

He spent the rest of that night dozing in a chair at the Infirmary while he waited to see how Clare came out of the anæsthetic.

'She was lucky it missed her lung, and she's young and strong—she'll be fine,' the doctor told him. But he waited all the same.

He had killed a man and all he felt was relief that Carrick was dead. It was like putting down a mad dog, but all the same, a man was not a dog. And the anger was still there, that Clare and David had been threatened and he himself had gone through so much, for what? It didn't feel as if it was all over because there was no reason for it to have happened. The futility of it kept sleep at bay. Maybe when it was only an episode in the past he might be able to think it all out rationally, but for now the anger festered away inside him and he was glad he'd killed Carrick.

The wooden arms of the chair cut into his bruised ribs each time he shifted position and the perished leather of the seat creaked if he moved. The hours passed slowly and the scenario of Carrick dropping into the sea was repeated over and over in his mind. He wondered if they'd found his body.

'We'll tackle that in daylight,' Jamieson said as Jane Freeman was led away weeping. John wondered if she was crying for her dead lover or because he'd deserted her to face the music all by herself. He didn't much care. David had fallen asleep in his arms, too exhausted even to take an interest in the police activities.

'God, John, you look awful,' Tollis said, and Jamieson offered to send him in a police car to be checked over.

'I must see how Clare is,' he said. 'And that woman gave David some sort of tablet to make him sleep, so I'll take him to the hospital with me.'

Jamieson walked to the patrol car with him. 'Statements can wait, I've enough to be going on with,' he said as his men boarded *Sea Princess* to take her fittings apart. And then he'd added one more sentence that took away all John's relief that the affair was finally over.

'One of my men is with the young lady to see she comes to no further harm.'

He saw John's expression and spelled out the rest.

'We don't know if Carrick was acting for himself or if Scott put him up to this, so we're not taking any chances. I'm very sorry that Carrick slipped away from us to get this far.'

John noted the 'us'—Jamieson was not passing the buck to his men but accepting the blame himself.

He'd seen David checked over and put in the children's ward for the night. 'Whatever it was, the effects have worn off,' the doctor said, looking at him suspiciously and no wonder. A man who had obviously been beaten up, arrived with a young boy who had been doped, but the police constable with John had explained some of the circumstances.

A nurse brought him a cup of tea at around 4.0 a.m. and the news that Clare was sleeping peacefully. 'You can see for yourself if you like.'

And for what was left of that long night, John sat beside Clare's bed, watching the drip run into the back of her hand. He couldn't take his eyes off her because he knew it could all have turned out so differently. She was still very pale but her fingers were warm in his hand. In the corridor a police sergeant of forty-plus was on guard. He looked like an ex-boxer, a steady man with a world-weary expression, and when John slipped out of the room just after seven, he knew Clare was in safe hands.

He looked in at Rees before leaving the hospital and was told that Rees was resting comfortably. 'He's to have a by-pass and then he'll—hopefully—be able to lead a normal life,' the nurse said. She too eyed John's battered face and stained clothes but said nothing. John looked through the glass partition at Rees but didn't go into the room. Rees would never be normal again, not with Toby's death on his conscience.

Gwen had arrived when he got to the Sentinel office and she looked bewildered and upset. Sipping Tollis's bitter coffee that did nothing to take away the sour taste in his mouth, John told her not to worry about David. 'He's fine and can come home later this morning.'

'I'd gone to collect his photographs when that woman came,' she said angrily. 'He was so keen to see how they turned out.' And she reached into her bag and brought out a bundle of envelopes containing the developed prints.

'You can take them to him when you collect him,' John said gently. His whole body was one vast ache and he had not yet inspected his bruises. His clothes were stained with Clare's blood, crumpled and dirty, and he was too tired to climb the stairs to Rees's flat to soak in the bath.

'What was Jamieson doing when you left?'

'Aiming to bring Scott in, I think.' Tollis scratched his unshaven chin.

'He's not likely to admit anything, though, and he did tell you that Carrick had been doing the blundering around.'

'I'm going to see Gumley,' John said, blinking the gritty feeling from his eyes. 'I'll have a shower and change and then drive over there. Maybe he'll tie up some loose ends.'

'There's no need. Jamieson has something to get his teeth into now and he's not going to be put off just because Gumley's sick.'

Gwen had opened the packets of prints and was idly looking through them, when suddenly she smiled. 'David will be pleased. You've ruined some of your snaps and his are much better.' She passed a couple over to John who was not really in the mood to look at them.

'See?' she said. And he did see . . . photographs that he certainly had not taken. Gumley's house was in the background and there were various shots of men leaving it. Whoever had held the camera had indeed cut off important bits but in one Garek was standing grim-faced in the doorway looking at the departing backs of Tony Scott and another man whose head was missing. In the next, the mysterious man was revealed as Carrick, climbing into Scott's car.

And then John knew exactly what he was seeing. He passed the photographs to Tollis without a word. Tollis studied them and then looked up, puzzled.

'It's what they've been looking for, a roll of undeveloped film,' John explained. 'Toby must have dropped it into the carrier that had David's present in it and it just got mixed up with the other spools. It's been safe in a chemist's shop all along.' He looked again and saw that in the background of one there was a car that had Rees's number plate. So his uncle hadn't just sent Toby, he'd been there himself.

'Toby must have had the camera hidden in some way,' Tollis said. 'That would explain the bad shots, but someone spotted him.'

And that sealed his fate, but it still didn't explain anything. Why was the spool of film so important that Scott, or Carrick, had killed Toby when they couldn't get it?

'What the hell does it mean?' he asked irritably.

Tollis reached for the phone. 'I'll try to reach Jamieson and then I'll send one of the men over there with the prints. Maybe he'll be able to solve it.'

The morning dragged. John took a shower and let the

needles of hot water pound his bruises and then joined
Tollis for something to eat while Tollis chain-smoked. They
knew that Jamieson had received the prints but so far there
was no word from him, and in the end John went off to sit
with Clare again because the inaction was driving him mad.

She had colour in her cheeks now and incredibly was
keen to get out of bed to sit in a chair. 'I didn't feel the
bullet going in,' she said with a smile, 'but now I feel as if
a horse has kicked me.' And the pain was there in her eyes.
She knew the rest of it now, and the news of Carrick's death
had been accepted calmly. 'But it's over—and for Arran
Sinclair as well.'

John hadn't given that side of it a thought, but he wondered now if Arran would still end up with Scott for a
neighbour.

'Except for some loose ends,' he said. Like whose gun
killed Toby Cairns and why was Rees at Gumley's with
Scott and Carrick?

Jamieson arrived at the Sentinel offices in the middle of
the afternoon and reported that the gun had been recovered
from the sea but as yet no body had been found. 'It was a
.22 Smith and Wesson, semi-automatic, the same one that
killed your man. Scott is being questioned but he's not
saying anything, claims he knows nothing about what Carrick got up to. I'm off to see Albert Gumley and I thought
Mr Leith might like to come along—he deserves that much
—and it might just make his father-in-law open up for us.'

John had never been in Gumley's bedroom but that was
where the conference with his father-in-law took place. He
was propped up on lots of pillows and an oxygen cylinder
was beside the bed, but John found it hard to feel any
sympathy for him. The man was a shell, wasted away to
skin and bone, yet there was no mistaking the dislike he felt
for John, even now.

'I knew nothing of Scott at first,' Gumley said. 'I asked

Kramer to find an attractive property for me to buy.' He ignored John's gasp of surprise and continued as if he knew he could only speak for so long and wanted to get it all out. 'Kramer wasn't interested at first until I told him it was for my grandson's birthday present. Then he said there was a parcel of land for sale that would be ideal for redeveloping —I found out that he was sentimental about the place but it seemed a good investment.' He paused for breath and Garek looked anxious but Gumley was determined to finish.

'We did a little digging and discovered that Carrick was selling the land to pay off debts to Scott, who wasn't all that keen to take over the whole investment. He just wanted a flat strip along the river, so I agreed that they should come here and discuss the whole thing.' Gumley smiled. 'Kramer involved with a drug dealer? No, he didn't know that then, or even that Scott was in the background, but Kramer *did* know that I was changing my investments for my grandson's birthday present. Yes, those papers I gave you, Mr Leith, you really should have read them carefully. But Kramer didn't trust Carrick, so he brought that young man along here to keep an eye on the comings and goings.'

He took a fit of shallow coughing that brought Garek to the bed to administer the oxygen. John and Jamieson waited patiently until Gumley's breathing improved but soon the old man waved the mask away.

'I bought the leisure complex; Scott only wanted the strip and concessions for his personal guests—I knew what he was about and I would have dealt with him in due course . . . or my good friend Garek would.' Garek nodded his bald head ominously. 'But—' and this Gumley was obviously enjoying; he kept them waiting for a long minute before continuing—'but the bit I really liked was that I put it all in your name, Mr Leith, to be passed to the boy when he was of age. It is all legally correct, as you would have seen if you'd not tossed those papers aside so casually.'

'You stupid bastard, do you know what you did? Carrick kidnapped David and nearly killed him. I don't want the land—David will never own the land. I'll see that Arran Sinclair gets it back, complete with your luxury bungalows and saunas . . .'

Gumley was staring at him, his hooded eyes expressionless, but the gaping mouth told its own story. Garek reached for the mask again.

'I don't know why they killed that stupid novice,' he gasped.

Jamieson spoke for the first time. 'I do. According to statements made by Scott, he was in the Bahamas at the time a young woman was murdered in Glasgow and someone did indeed use his passport to fly there. Toby's photographs destroy that alibi and, ironically, Scott may well be charged as an accomplice in that young man's murder as well. We've got him on both counts.'

'And Mr Leith has him for a partner,' Gumley said with a flash of malice. John had had enough and turned to leave but Gumley spoke again. 'The boy. I didn't want to involve the boy.'

John kept going and didn't look back. One day, maybe quite soon now, David would inherit Gumley's home and his wealth and, as the old man had delighted in pointing out, he would also inherit Gumley's genes. But Trish had had her father's genes and she'd turned out all right. David would too. It was over.

'The future?' Tollis asked later. 'I need you here—we make a good team.'

'No way.'

Tollis didn't seem put off. 'Take a look at yourself. You haven't complained once about the punishment you've taken. You came back ready for more every time Carrick did his damnedest. I need men who sink their teeth into the job and won't let go.'

'I was scared stiff most of the time,' John pointed out, but Tollis shrugged.

'I'd have thought you thick if you weren't. At least think it over.'

So he did. If Rees came back to run Kramer's, that meant he'd be free to return to his old office, to pick up the life he'd had before and he knew that was impossible. Then he remembered the undercurrent of excitement he'd felt for the past couple of weeks and he recognized that there was something irresistible about Tollis's proposal.

Tollis lit another cigarette and grinned.